BILLY THE KID
(A YEAR IN THE LIFE OF)

By
REG BENNETT

Illustrated by Peter Revell

ASHRIDGE PRESS

Published by Ashridge Press
A subsidiary of Country Books
Courtyard Cottage, Little Longstone, Bakewell, Derbyshire DE45 1NN
Tel/Fax: 01629 640670
e-mail: dickrichardson@country-books.co.uk

ISBN 1 901214 58 3

© 2006 Reg Bennett
© 2006 Peter Revell (Illustrations)

The rights of Reg Bennett as author of this work have
been asserted by him in accordance with the
Copyright, Designs and Patents Act 1993.

All rights reserved. No part of this publication may be reproduced,
stored in a retrieval system, or transmitted, in any way or form, or by
any means, electronic, mechanical, photocopying, or otherwise,
without the prior permission of the author and publisher.

British Library Cataloguing in Publication Data.
A catalogue record for this book is available from the British Library.

Printed and bound by:
Antony Rowe Ltd. Eastbourne

Dedication

For my wife, Pam,
and, for their valuable input,
Jenny Edgar, Janette Sykes, Peter Revell
and Brian James.

1938

BURBAGE, A PEAKLAND VILLAGE IN
DERBYSHIRE.
BILLY IS TEN.

Chapter One

WESLEY'S BOIL

High elation ran through Billy. It was 4 o'clock on a Friday afternoon. He was just out of school. While he chased a dead leaf down the gully of the school toilet to the drain hole with a jet of straining urine, he was thinking of his friend, Wesley Ward. Wesley hadn't been to school for four days. Billy wondered if the School Inspector had been round to Wesley's house wanting to know why Wesley was off school, because his own mum always threatened him with a visit from the School Inspector if he wanted to shy off school.

The pressure on his bladder now relieved Billy sighed, shook his willy and tucked it away behind the flies of his short, patched corduroy trousers; thankful he had not wet himself in class. He should have asked to 'go' he knew – as his mum always told him to – but the girls giggled behind their hands when he did that. If there was one thing be couldn't abide, it was giggling girls. It wouldn't be so had if they giggled when other boys asked to 'go', but no, they just seemed to pick on him. Perhaps it was because they sensed it acutely embarrassed him to ask to 'go'? He was never very good at hiding his feelings, or so his mum said,

But this wasn't finding out what was wrong with Wesley Ward. Maybe he should have made time in the week to go round to Wesley's house to ask how he was. But after finishing his evening newspaper round and having his tea and then doing his occasional stick-chopping-and-bundling job for a penny an hour at the sawmill, it proved to be near impossible. And on top of that, his mother always insisted he be in by half past eight sharp or he would risk feeling her dolly stick.

Billy stared at the black painted concrete toilet wall in front him. It was covered with yellow stains. When he asked his granddad what caused the marks his granddad asked him if the water sprays worked. When he said only occasionally his granddad replied, 'So there you are, then,' but didn't elaborate further which confused and disappointed Billy a little.

But now he wrinkled his nose at the smell rising from the gully. For sure, he didn't know how Joe 'Piggy' Piggott and his mates could stand in here during playtime, smoking dog ends of Woodbine cigarettes and spitting and thinking they were big when they weren't! They must have no sense of smell at all. But then, he decided, standing here thinking of these things was making him no better than them, nor was it helping him to find out what was wrong with Wesley Ward.

Spurred by the reminder he ran out of the School Toilet, across the playground and out on to Dolly Peg Row and headed towards Wesley's house.

He was approaching Christ Church, Burbage when he saw Wesley. He was sitting on the church wall, by the church gates. He was resting his boots on top of the green-painted Buxton Corporation seat, which the old people of the village used every day to sit on and gossip. But at the moment nobody was there, apart from Wesley.

When he got close he couldn't help but stare at Wesley's clearly unhappy, pixie-like face. Wesley's skin was usually a healthy pale pink but today it seemed to have the texture and colour of bread dough. Billy also noticed Wesley was holding his head on one side in a peculiarly stiff-necked way. Also, his eyes lacked their usual twinkle.

'Now then, Wesley,' he said, as cheerfully as he could seeing as his mate looked so glum, 'art' all right?'

Wesley squinted at him, the pain he was suffering clearly reflected in his eyes. 'No, I'm not.'

Billy frowned. 'Why; what's up?'

Wesley pointed, 'Can't you see?'

Billy peered round at the other side of Wesley's neck and saw the large boil plaster stuck on it. But that wasn't surprising, Billy decided, because Wesley always seemed to have one or more boils maturing on some part of his anatomy. But this particular boil was enormous. Indeed, it looked so inviting Billy felt compelled to jump up on top of the wall so he could have a closer inspection of the angry, yellow-tipped apex poking out of the hole in the top of the plaster.

'You've got a bad one there,' he said, after the examination. 'Is that why you've been off school?'

His friend groaned and looked really pitiful – almost close to tears. 'Had no sleep for four days with it,' he moaned. 'I don't know where to put me head when I go to bed, it hurts so much.'

Billy put on his best sympathy face. 'Aye, I know what you mean.' At times he suffered from boils. To try and cure them his mum always forced him to drink Dandelion Tea to purify his blood, also gulp down California Syrup of Figs to make him go to the toilet to clear his bowels. Sometimes, she coated the boils with Blue Gentian, which, according to some, was also supposed to be very good.

'Have you been to t' doctor with it?" he said.

Wesley looked at him forlornly. 'Doctors? Who can afford doctors? You've got to be near dead before you can afford doctors.'

Billy raised his brows. 'Aye,' he said, with feeling, 'me mum never likes taking me to the doctors, because they cost too much.'

'So there you are then,' said Wesley mournfully.

Now deeply moved by Wesley's obvious despair, and wanting to do something about it, Billy found the usual flood of ideas coursing through his constantly active brain. Indeed, some of the gang said he was so fall of bright ideas it was a pity some of them didn't work occasionally.

'Have you tried Potters Healing and Drawing Ointment?' he said. 'It's a penny a tin at the Heath and Heather place down Buxton. Me granddad swears by it. He says there's comfrey in it and comfrey's very good for owt like that.'

Wesley shook his head. 'No, I haven't. Me dad put a kaolin poultice on it last night but it throbbed so much I took it off as soon as I got to bed.' Wesley's look became even gloomier. 'I didn't tell me dad though; he would have whaled the hide off me if I had. I just told him it must have come off during the ni–'

Wesley stopped mid-sentence and hissed, 'Hey up, here comes Monica Pane.'

Made instantly on guard Billy turned as unobtrusively as he could. A glance told him Monica was approaching from the direction of St John's Road and, at this moment, was passing the bus stop for Buxton. She was licking a halfpenny raspberry lollipop. Billy immediately deduced she must have got it from the Post Office on Macclesfield Road as soon as she came out of school. She seemed, he thought with some jealousy, to have money for everything did Monica Pane.

Monica was now staring at them with those sharp, inquisitive blue eyes of hers. Today her ginger hair – usually in ringlets – hung straight and limp, nearly brushing the top of her shoulders. It was held off her forehead by a tortoiseshell Alice band. The freckles on her nose and cheeks, Billy noticed, were very pronounced today. His mum said she was a tomboy, whatever that was.

When she got close Monica frowned and then glared at him. 'So,' she said. 'What are you gawping at. Billy Nobstick?'

Though stung. Billy quickly regained his composure. 'I don't know what it is,' he said. He smirked and nudged his pal, 'How about you, Wesley?'

'Nor me.' said Wesley, coming to life and grinning, clearly not wanting to look a pansy in front of Monica and able to manage the pain he was suffering. 'It looks like summat t' cat's brought in.'

Instantly, Monica's face went peevish and her chin came up and she glared down her snub nose at them with angry eyes. Then she aimed her stare at Wesley and snapped, 'You didn't say that last Saturday, up in the Horseshoe Plantation on Cavendish Golf Course, Wesley Ward.'

Wesley looked indignant. 'So what? Nowt come of it.'

Monica's eyes rounded and she looked even more waspish, 'Nowt, eh? So I can tell me mum then – if it were *nowt*.'

'You wouldn't,' Wesley breathed, clearly shocked.

Monica swayed her hips and smirked. 'I might,' she said.

'Anyway, shouldn't you be at home? You've been off school all week. It doesn't say because it's Friday and school's finished you can be out playing, if you've been *poorly*.'

Monica took a swipe at her lollipop with her tongue and then continued, 'I could tell me mum, and she could tell the School Inspector. Then what would you do, Wesley Ward?'

'You wouldn't,' Wesley repeated, with even more emphasis.

Now puzzled, because he didn't know what was going on. Billy stared at Monica. It was odd behaviour from her anyway 'You're up to summat, Monica Pane,' he said, 'what is it?'

Monica looked coy and took another lick at her lollipop. Then she said, 'You and the gang are going up to that camp you've built in Big Bushy in Grin Wood tonight, aren't you?'

'What if we are?' Billy said.

Monica tilted her chin. 'I want to come,' she said.

Billy cut air with his grubby hand. 'Well, you can forget that,' he said, 'we don't want girls with us. What do you say, Wesley?'

'Yeh – forget that,' said Wesley, but he was frowning his confusion at Billy. Billy guessed he was doing that because Wesley didn't know the gang were going to Big Bushy in Grin Wood tonight... until now.

Monica's stare was even more spiteful. 'If you don't let me come,' she said, 'I'll tell about me and Wesley Ward in Horseshoe Plantation.'

Billy turned to Wesley. 'What's she on about, pal?'

'It were nowt,' said Wesley. 'She's just being stupid.'

Billy turned to Monica. 'Well, if Wesley says it were nowt, then it were nowt and you can forget all about Big Bushy. Anyway, girls smell.'

Monica's freckled face opened in indignant amazement. 'Did you say girls *smell?*'

'Yeh,' said Billy and grinned, oafishly. 'In fact,' he added, 'they smell awful.' He nudged Wesley. 'Isn't that right, pal?'

'They smell like a baby's cot,' said Wesley.

Monica arched her neck and leaned forward and put her hands on her hips. 'It's boys who *smell*,' she declared. 'They smell disgusting.'

Billy grinned his triumph as his trap worked. 'Oh?' he said 'In that case, what d'you want to play with us for?'

'Yeh,' Wesley tittered gleefully, 'chew on that.'

For moments Monica stood there, looking as though she was going to burst any minute, then she said,

'If you don't let me come with you I will tell what you said to me on the Cavendish Golf Course, Wesley Ward, and I will tell me mum you're playing out when you've been off school all week and she'll tell the School Inspector.'

'So what?' Wesley said. 'Me mum's already told him.'

Monica stamped her foot and began to look desperate. 'I only want to play,' she said. 'I can do anything you lot can do.'

'You're still not coming,' Billy said.

'So put that in your pipe and smoke it,' Wesley said.

Once more Monica looked as though she was about to explode then she stamped her foot and said, 'Sod you.'

She turned and stalked up Macclesfield Old Road.

When it was clear she wasn't coming back Wesley returned to looking miserable and gingerly fingered the area of his neck where the boil was. However, made intensely curious by what had gone before; Billy leered a grin at him and said, 'So, what's this about you and Monica Pane in Horseshoe Plantation, eh?'

Wesley gave him a sour look. 'You might as well know, I suppose. It was nowt, like I said. You went to help your granddad dig his allotment remember? The gang went to the pictures down Buxton. I'd got no money so I decided to go and look for golf balls on the golf course so I could sell them on. It was my luck to have Monica Pane latch on to me when I was walking down Nursery Lane. I told her to bugger off but you know what she's like – just trails along behind until you have to let her come.'

'Yeh, I do,' said Billy, with feeling.

'Anyway,' Wesley said, 'when we got on to the golf links we didn't have much luck looking in the rough grass so Monica said let's try Horseshoe Plantation,' Wesley sighed. 'We hadn't been in there a couple of minutes when she said she was tired and wanted to sit down. Though I wanted to get on I sat down with her. But I soon got fed up with that so I said I'd show her mine if she'd show me hers. I thought it might scare her off and I could search for golf balls properly.'

Billy said, 'And did it?'

'No,' said Wesley miserably, 'just the opposite. She seemed keen. You know what she's like sometimes.'

'So?' Billy said. 'What happened?'

'Some golfers came along.'

'And that were it?' Billy said.

'Yes,' said Wesley.

'So it really were nowt?'

'That's what I've been telling you,' Wesley said. Now he looked askance, 'So, what's this about you and the gang going up to Big Bushy tonight?'

Billy said, 'Be there at six o'clock, if you feel up to it.'

'Oh, I'll be up to it,' Wesley said. 'I'm fed up of me mum telling me to get from under her feet and stop moaning.'

'So, that's it then,' said Billy,

'Yeh,' Wesley went back to looking miserable again.

Billy jumped down off the wall. 'Do you fancy coming to help me do me newspaper round?'

Wesley shook his head. 'I can't. I've got to be in for half past four to get me plaster changed.'

Billy said, 'See you tonight then?'

'Yeh,' said Wesley.

Leaving his best friend. Billy cantered off towards Mr Belham's lock up shop, out of which Mr Belham sold news-papers and magazines. But there was no need to hurry, he decided. This week it was Piggy Piggott's turn to fetch the evening newspapers from Buxton LMS station. All he needed to do was wait for Piggy returning so he could make up his newspaper round and deliver it before going home for his tea. However, he liked chatting to Mr Belham, so he didn't mind getting to the shop early. Maybe he could get some advice from Mr Belham about Wesley's boil? But, after some silent deliberation he decided not to ask.

It was twenty past six o'clock when Billy finally reached Big Bushy, the huge beech tree they used as the Greenwood Tree, deep in Grin Wood. The gang all reckoned it would pass for Robin Hood's fabled oak any time and Grin Wood was definitely Sherwood Forest

As he walked up the rise to Big Bushy he saw the gang was already there and that a wood fire was blazing brightly within the ring of small limestone rocks they used to contain it.

The gang, Billy observed, were gathered around Wesley, who was sitting on the dead tree bole they used for a seat. They were studying Wesley's boil with great interest. Wesley, Billy decided, as he got close, was a picture of misery.

He said, 'How are you feeling, pal?'

Wesley groaned as he looked up. 'Worse, if owt.'

Winker Benton – dumpy and fat faced – stepped back from inspecting the angry swelling and stammered, 'W - well, I - I'd say it w-were r-ready for b-bursting.' Winker blinked rapidly as he talked.

Lanky, thin faced Eddie Green, while poking the potato he was baking in the fire with a long stick, said, 'I'll go along with that.'

'It's a right mess,' said Percy Green, Eddie Green's younger brother by a year and as short as Eddie was long.

'You can say that again,' said Hump Bramble, nodding his plump, freckled, sandy-topped head and shrugging his humpback shoulders.

Winker Benton, now squinting at Wesley with interest, said, 'W- what are your f- folks doing a - about it, Wesley?'

'T' usual stuff,' moaned Wesley, 'kaolin poultices and boil plasters.'

Hump Bramble said, 'Why don't they take you to that Welfare Clinic on Bridge Street down Buxton?'

Wesley stared, horrified. 'No way. I'm not going there. They do all sorts of things to you down there.'

'Well, summat's got to be done,' Billy said.

'What, for instance?' groaned Wesley, staring up at him. 'Don't say you've got another of your bright ideas?'

Feeling a little put out by that Billy paused to kick the dead copper-coloured beech leaves under his hobnailed boots. But he decided to ignore the hurting, scathing remark. It was clear Wesley wasn't himself.

'If you must know,' he said, 'it's not my idea, It's Owd Isaac's.'

A collective gasp went up from the gang and Wesley groaned, 'Not him.' Despite his boil, he shook his head vigorously. 'No way, mate.'

Billy said, 'Why? What's up with Owd Isaac?'

'He's barmy, for one thing,' said Eddie Green.

'A tramp for another,' said Percy.

Collective laughter went up into the leaf-nude canopy overhead and Billy glared. 'He's nowt of the sort. He's all right is Owd Isaac. He got four medals in the Great War and he's the best poacher around.'

Owd Isaac also lived in a shed in Grin Wood and kept hens and did odd jobs about the village: emptying bucket toilets and drystone walling and digging gardens and all sorts of things.

'G - getting b - back to the b - boil,' Winker Benton said, 'if it d - doesn't b - burst soon, it'll have to be l - lanced. That's what me m - mum said last night and s - she should know, she's a n - nurse.'

New worry lines etched Wesley's elfin face. 'Did you say lanced?'

'T- that's w - what me m - mum said.'

Wesley began rocking to and fro on the dead tree bole. 'I don't fancy having it lanced,' he said. 'No way.' He looked up at Billy, pleading in his eyes, 'What's this cure Owd Isaac was on about?'

'He said to bottle it,' Billy said.

Wesley frowned. 'What's that supposed to mean?'

'You get a bottle,' explained Billy, 'tip boiling water into the bottom, get it red hot then empty the water out, cool the neck end and put it over the boil.'

Wesley stared at him as though he was from a foreign country.

'Put a red hot bottle on your neck?'

'You cool the top first,' said Billy.

'You must think I'm barmy!' Wesley said.

Eddie Green, turning the potato he was baking in the fire, said, 'Well, it's better than having it lanced. I had an abscess on me arm lanced last year. It were awful. They cut across it and then squeeze out all the matter. Ugh! Great yellow globs of the stuff and there were blood all over t' place.'

'Shut up, will you?' Wesley howled.

Eddie looked hurt. 'I were only trying to help,' he said.

'Well don't bother,' said Wesley.

Billy said, 'Don't say you're scared, Wesley.'

Wesley glared at him. 'No, I'm not scared,' he said, 'but I'm not daft either.'

Winker Benton said, 'Well, I - I know where there's an e - empty D - Dandelion and B - Burdock bottle. It's stuck in the wall - just above the Recreation Ground. I'll g-go and f - fetch it if you like.'

'Hang on a minute,' said Wesley. 'I haven't agreed yet.'

But, to Billy's satisfaction, Winker was already running down the wood. And Eddie Green was picking up the kettle they used to boil water in to brew tea in the old aluminium teapot Winker's mum gave them. He shook it. He seemed to take it for granted the operation going ahead.

'Empty,' he said, 'and I can't fetch any, I've got this potato to watch.' He prodded the potato he was baking to illustrate his point.

'I'll fetch some,' Billy said. 'There's that barrel by the side of Welmet's hen cote, near Grin Quarry Tips.'

'It'll be mucky,' Wesley protested.

'We'll boil it first,' said Billy. 'Me granddad said boiling water kills all germs. That's what they did in the Trenches. Boil it.'

'Oh, aye, thee grandfather,' said Wesley, with some disdain. 'He's always saying summat is thee grandfather.'

Billy again put the unkind words down to Wesley's painful condition and went running off down the wood. Within ten minutes he was back with the kettle full of water. A couple of minutes later Winker Benton came trotting in, carrying the empty Dandelion and Burdock bottle.

As soon as he saw the bottle Wesley said, 'I haven't agreed yet.'

Billy said, 'You don't want it lanced, do you, Wesley?'

'No, but...'

'You want to let it burst, then?'

'No, but...' Wesley groaned. 'Better get on with it, I suppose.'

Billy bedded the kettle in the fire Eddie Green had built up while he was gone. After a few minutes, the kettle lid began to rattle.

Hump Bramble said, looking round, 'Who's going to do it?'

'B - Billy,' said Winker unhesitatingly, lifting the boiling kettle off the fire, using a piece of old carpet, 'it w - were his idea.'

Billy found the announcement hit him like a ton weight. In all the excitement he didn't give a thought as to who would actually do the operation. But, like Winker said, it was his idea. Another thing: Wesley was his best friend. Who else could it be but him?

He picked up the Dandelion and Burdock bottle from where Winker dropped it. Shutting out any further reservations he possessed, he wedged it between two stones and took the kettle of boiled water off Winker and began to pour it into the vessel. The gang crowded round, their eagerness almost like a live animal.

'Get back a bit,' he said.

They did, but only a fraction.

When there was enough water in the bottom of the bottle Billy looked down at Wesley.

'Are you ready, pal?' he said,

Wesley moaned, looked up. 'Don't you have to take the plaster off first?'

Billy offered his pal a sickly grin. 'Oh, aye. I forgot.'

Winker Benton said, stepping forward, 'L - let me t - take it off. Me mum s - showed me h - how to t - take off p - plasters. I'm an e - expert.'

Before anybody could say otherwise, he took hold of a loose edge of the plaster and, with one snatch, ripped it off.

Wesley's reaction was instant. With a huge howl he leapt into the air and began running around the huge girth of Big Bushy, holding the back of his neck. 'Ow, ow, ow! You rotten bugger, Benton!'

Billy chased after him 'Hang on, Wesley, we've got to get this bottle on before it goes cold.'

'He needn't have done that,' Wesley said, glaring. But he stopped running and sat down on the tree bole and stretched his neck out. 'Go on then,' he said, 'if you're going to do it; but go careful. Not like him.' He glared painfully at Winker.

As gently as he could Billy pressed the neck of the bottle over the boil and held it down.

For a second or two nothing seemed to happen, then the neck of the bottle tightened on Wesley's neck, as if it was rivetting itself to the inflamed flesh.

After moments, Wesley leapt into the air. 'Ow! Ow! Ow! Get it off. Billy! Get the bugger off!'

He began racing round Big Bushy once more, clawing wildly at the pop bottle attached to his neck, clearly wanting to tear it away. Equably as anxious to keep it there. Billy chased with him hanging on to it and yelling, 'Leave it on, Wesley!'

Now Wesley began racing down the grassy bank, falling away from Big Bushy to the flat piece of ground at the bottom. Following on, whooping like a pack of Red Indians, the gang bounded down after them

It was about this time that Billy saw blood and corruption come spurting into the bottle from the boil's fearsome head. It was splattering the glass sides. It looked disgusting. But it worked like magic on Wesley. He stopped shouting and came to a halt.

'It's bust, pal,' he said, his eyes wide, 'the bloody thing's bust!'

Wesley was the only one in the gang who swore properly. Billy knew it made him extremely popular with all the gang.

But gleeful the treatment had worked, he yelled above the shouts of the gang, "What did I tell thee? Owd Isaac were right.'

Wesley was obviously too euphoric to answer.

Billy let the corruption-filled bottle fall to the ground and it revealed the hole that once held the core of Wesley's boil. To his horror, he saw blood was pouring out of it.

'Get your hanky on your neck quick, Wesley,' he yelled. 'You're bleeding like a stuck pig!'

'I haven't got one,' wailed Wesley. New terror filled his stare, 'Oh heck, me mum'll whale me the hide off me if I mess up me coat and shirt.'

Winker Benton began fumbling in his right trouser pocket and pulled out a piece of old shirttail. 'H - here, p - put this o - on it, Wesley,' he said.

Wesley took the piece of material and pressed it against his bloody neck and everything suddenly seemed to calm down.

Eddie Green speared the potato he was baking and lifted it out of

the fire and inspected it. He grinned and said,
'Done to a turn.'
'Dost want to get home, Wesley?' Billy said.
Wesley nodded. 'I do feel a bit groggy.'

There was an air of achievement about the gang as they stamped out the fire and began trooping down Grin Wood. But after a few steps Winker Benton stopped. 'H - hang on,' he said, 'that D - dandelion and B- burdock bottle I f- fetched. I were going to t - take it b -back the T - top Shop to get a p - penny on it.'

Eddie Green stared as though Winker had turned a bit weird. 'You can't take it back with all that stuff in it?'

'B - ut it's a p - penny,' protested Winker. 'I c - can wash it o - out.'

He went down the bank and gingerly picked the bottle up. Everybody said, 'Ugh,' and Wesley added, 'Dirty bugger, Benton.'

Winker glared up at them, then seemed to relent 'A - all right, I won't.' He threw the bottle down on to the grass again.

Eddie Green began cutting his baked potato in two with his penknife. The job done he turned to Wesley. 'Here, get this down thee neck, Wesley,' he said, offering him a half. 'I'd have been messing in me keks (trousers) if Billy had done that to me.'

Wesley took the half-potato with the hand that wasn't holding the cloth to his bleeding neck put it in his mouth and began munching. Warmth filled Billy. This was what the gang was all about.

He sighed happily and looked up. The last rays of the setting April sun were splintering shafts of golden light through the swelling green buds of the canopy. The trees would soon be coming into leaf.

He draped an arm across Wesley's narrow shoulders and grinned. 'Boils, mate,' he said, 'nowt to 'em, eh?'

'Nowt,' Wesley said and returned the smile.

Laughs from all the gang rang down the Greenwood.

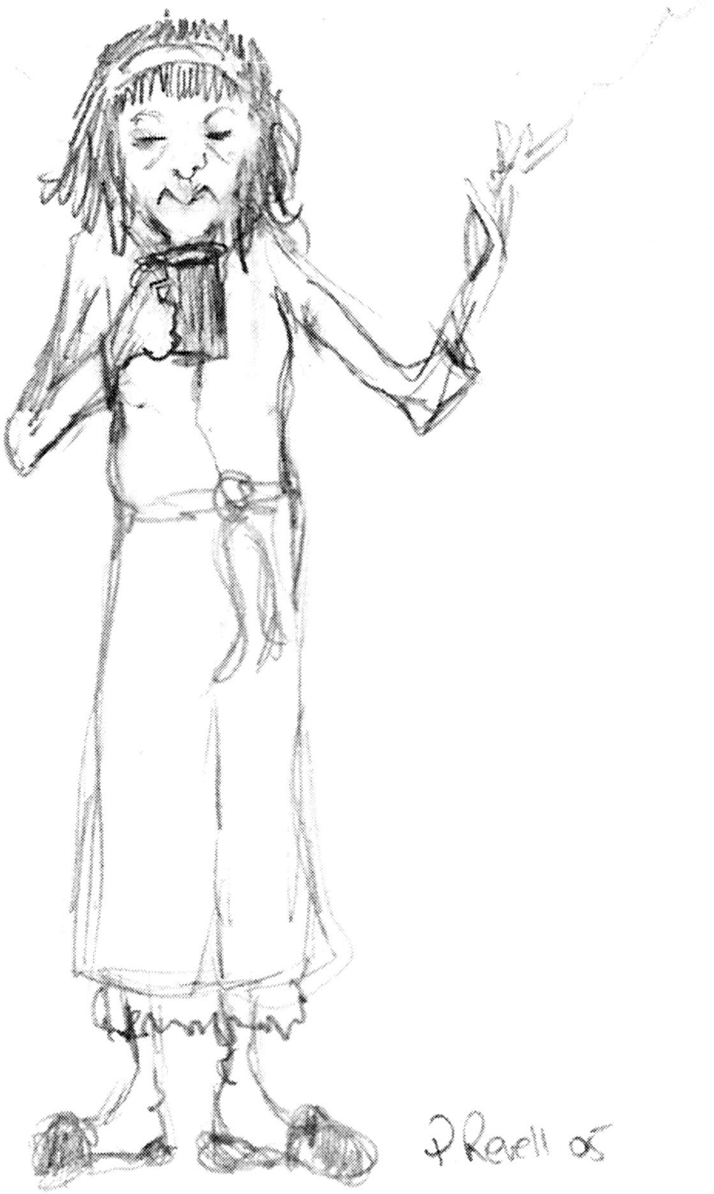
P Revell 05

CHAPTER TWO
POCKET MONEY

It was three weeks later and it was ten o'clock on a bright, warm Saturday morning in May. Billy was sitting on the pavement, his back lounging against Mr Ashburn's high, moss-covered limestone garden wall. He was staring across the road to where Hump Bramble lived. He was waiting patiently for Mrs Bramble to get up and draw the faded brown curtains that were spread across the big bay window of the large, semi-detached gritstone built house she and Hump lived in. But, also, he was casting glances at Piggy Piggott who was ambling towards him from the direction of St John's Road. Piggy had his hands in his trouser pockets and was kicking a tin can along the cobbled gutter. When he reached Billy he stopped and squinted down.

'Now then. Billy,' he said.

Billy picked his nose and considered the 'crow' he dislodged, balancing it on the end of his little finger. 'Now then.'

'What are t' waiting for?' Piggy said.

'Nowt.'

'Playing out?'

'No.'

'Oh,' Piggy raised his brows. 'Thought you might be, seeing as it's Saturday.'

'Well, I'm not,' said Billy. He flicked the 'crow' away.

'Waiting for Hump?' Piggy said presently.

'I might be.'

Piggy squinted and looked exasperated. You couldn't have got out of bed the wrong side because you were all right when we were making up our newspaper rounds this morning."

'Don't feel like talking, that's all,' said Billy.

'That's a new one,' Piggy said. 'Well, I'll see thee.' He went away muttering about miserable buggers with nowt to do.

After watching him depart Billy once more returned his gaze to Mrs Bramble's big bay window. This was all about Pocket Money and nowt to do with Piggy Piggott. It was complicated, too. What he earned from his newspaper round and his sticking-chopping-and-bundling job all went towards the housekeeping. He didn't get a penny out of it. Indeed if it weren't for Mrs Bramble wanting her shopping done on a Saturday morning he would have nothing at all to spend, unless he tapped his granddad for a copper or two, which he didn't like to do. However, the money situation wasn't all doom and gloom. Occasionally, his friend Owd Isaac asked him to clean out his hen cotes and usually gave him sixpence for doing a good job. But it wasn't a regular thing.

He reared up when he saw the curtains to Mrs Bramble's big bay window flicker and gradually part to reveal the good lady standing there in her shabby green dressing gown. As usual the perennial Park Drive cigarette was dangling from her lips,

She blinked her squinty eyes as she peered out at the sunny morning and surveyed the sun-drenched street.

First she looked up, then down. When her gaze rested on him, she smiled and gave him a little wave. Billy grinned and waved back because he liked Mrs Bramble, even though some people said she was a penny short of a shilling. But she was all right as far as he was concerned – the essence of kindness in fact.

He stared at her heart shaped, pale face. Her brown hair hung down around her thin neck like straggly rat-tails. However, she contrived to keep the hair out of her eyes by using a tortoiseshell Alice band. He thought: if there *was* anything odd about Mrs Bramble, it was her eyes. They were a strange, mottled, amber colour, not as Billy saw them very often because she squinted so much.

He got up off the pavement and ambled across the road, taking his time as he strolled up the tarmacadam garden path to Mrs Bramble's faded green back door.

Before he could knock, Mrs Bramble opened the door and smiled down at him saying, in her motherly way, 'Timothy's just got up. Billy, but he'll be ready shortly. Would you like to come through into the parlour while I get my order ready?'

'Yes,' Billy said.

The news that Timothy 'Hump' Bramble had 'just got up' didn't surprise Billy. In fact, he would have been surprised if Hump hadn't 'just got up.' As for Hump being 'ready shortly'. Billy doubted that very much as well, for Hump was never 'ready' – especially on a Saturday morning. But urged on by the thought of receiving reward for work well done, he followed Mrs Bramble across the familiar quarry-tiled floor of the big kitchen. Past the large, cast-iron gas-stove, past the rough, glazed stone sink with the one brass tap above it. Then past the small scrubbed deal table standing in the middle of the floor. As he entered the front room – or parlour as Mrs Bramble called it – Billy saw Hump was sitting in the chair with the back broken off. He was reading the Dandy comic and was picking his nose and inspecting the 'crow' before eating it. Hump didn't even bother to look up when he entered.

Now, as was his habit, Billy manoeuvred himself alongside the near-empty china cabinet, which was against the near wall, and then he looked at Mrs Bramble's worn Chesterfield armchair. As usual, it was drawn up in front of the large, black-leaded open range. The big range always attracted him, for the uprights were composed of white ceramic tiles, the centres of which were decorated with brilliant red roses.

Continuing to occupy himself he looked at the other pieces of furniture scattered about, even though they were familiar to him. He was just fascinated by the poverty of it all. There was the deal table standing in the rays of sunlight streaming in through the nets up to the big bay window. The table was covered with sheets of newspaper. Drawn up to the table were the two wooden dining chairs. They were painted chocolate brown, but the paint was very chipped and revealed the light-brown wood underneath.

Now he let his gaze stray to the orange box in the far corner. As usual the box – placed near the coalscuttle – was filled with sticks and newspapers, obviously there to kindle the fire with.

Newspaper sheets were scattered about the floor, too, to hide where the parquet-style lino was worn through. However, the thing that always drew Billy's attention most was the large gold-framed painting over the china cabinet. It was entitled 'Monarch of the Glen' and was painted by somebody called Sir Edwin Henry Landseer. The portrait was of a great stag with huge horns, standing defiantly on a hill in some heather. It seemed to be staring directly out of the picture at him.

These was no doubt about it: he loved it.

Now he watched, with some dread, as Mrs Bramble lighted another cigarette and shuffled in her worn black carpet slippers to the far side of the deal table, partly standing in the bow of the big bay window. On the table were a part-sliced loaf, a big wedge of yellow cheese and Mrs Bramble's King George the Fifth Coronation mug, filled with steaming hot tea. Beside the mug was an open tin of Nestlés Condensed Milk. He guessed Mrs Bramble had already stirred in a teaspoonful of the treacly liquid to lighten and sweeten her tea.

He watched her pick up the mug with her right hand, and then, with a flowing movement of her left hand, take the cigarette out of her mouth and exhale smoke across the sun's dazzling rays. It was like something Billy saw Bette Davis do in a picture at the Spa Cinema a month ago, except Miss Davis held her cigarette in a long holder.

Mrs Bramble began taking long slurping sips from the mug, while making quiet staccato coughing noises and rapidly blinking her squinty eyelids. She always did that, blink her eyelids when she drank tea, and Billy wondered if it was because she tried to drink the tea too hot. But she once told him: if there was one thing she liked more than anything in the world, it was the first cup of tea of the day. Perhaps that was why she couldn't wait for her tea to go cool, he thought

But knowing now he was in for a long wait Billy shifted his gaze to Hump. He was still in his nightshirt, was still reading his Dandy comic and his eyes were still swollen with sleep. And the beams of warm sunlight coming in through the big bay window behind him caused Hump's close-cropped hair to take on the appearance of fine sandpaper. The tuft of hair at the front, usually slicked back with solidified brilliantine, was, at the moment, splayed limply across his broad forehead.

Billy, turning to Mrs Bramble, said, as tactfully as he could, because he wanted to be out playing, 'Do you want much shopping done, Mrs Bramble?'

She smiled at him fondly. 'Oh, yes, quite a bit, Billy.' But then carried on sipping her tea and coughing and blinking.

Disappointed, Billy inwardly groaned. To fill in more time he now stared at the lump on Hump's back. Talk had it Hump was four years old. He was swinging on the coat hook that was screwed on to the back of the kitchen door. The hanger broke away and Hump partly dislocated his shoulder blade in the fall.

It was said Hump wouldn't go to the doctor with it created an almighty fuss about it and in the end Mrs Bramble didn't make him go, so the shoulder blade set that way. Some said the reason why she didn't make him go to the doctor's was Mrs Bramble lost her husband in a quarry accident only three weeks previous and she wasn't herself – and never was again if truth be known. Others just said Hump was spoiled rotten and he wanted his arse kicking. Others said Mrs Bramble couldn't afford to take him to the doctor's.

Billy said, more anxious now, 'Shall you be wanting your shopping done now, Mrs Bramble?'

Mrs Bramble said, 'Are you in a hurry, Billy?'

Billy wiped his nose on his jersey sleeve. 'I were just wondering?'

Mrs Bramble peered at him over the rim of her mug. 'I suppose you want to be out playing in this lovely sunshine, is that it?'

'Yes.'

Mrs Bramble smiled radiantly now. 'Of course you do,' she said in her motherly way and sedately put down her mug of tea.

Squinting her small eyes now, as if she had difficulty seeing, she shuffled across the floor on her ragged carpet slippers, which made funny slapping noises as she walked across the newspapers spread on the lino-covered flow. As she passed Hump she stroked his sandy hair and said, fondly,

'What do you want for breakfast, lovey?'

'Soft boiled eggs and some toast,' said Hump.

'I don't know about toast,' Mrs Bramble said, 'the fire isn't lit yet, but I'll see what I can do.'

'I want some toast,' Hump insisted.

'Oh, very well,' said Mrs Bramble. She turned and smiled. 'I hope you're not a fusspot like Timothy, hey. Billy?'

Billy self-consciously and stared at his feet. 'No,' he said.

He knew one thing for sure: if *he* talked to his mum like that he would get a real belt round the ear hole.

Mrs Bramble reached her purse from the mantelpiece and turned. 'Now, Billy,' she said, cheerfully, 'I want a Coburg loaf from Amos Goodfellow, two pounds of cheese – that nice Cheshire, tell him – and forty Park Drive cigarettes. Explain the cigarettes are for me. That will make it all right. Then from Phyllis Forwards I want five pounds of Lincoln potatoes, a spring cabbage, two pounds of carrots and a large swede.' She raised her thin brows then and stored at him. 'And make sure the cats haven't been on the vegetables, will you. Billy?'

Billy smiled and shuffled, a little embarrassed by that forthright statement even though Phyllis Forwards' shop did reek of cats. It was suspected the cats slept, or did worse, on the vegetables when the shop was shut. But his granddad said it was Phyllis Forwards' two tom cats that made the place smell, nothing else. She kept the shop clean enough did Phyllis, and, he added, she saw to it the cats didn't do any other mischief.

Mrs Bramble went into the kitchen. When she came back she was holding the usual large Hessian carrier bag. Billy knew she had made it out of an old sugar sack she got from the Co-op on Macclesfield Old Road. She couldn't afford anything else was his guess.

'There, that should hold them,' she said, beaming at him. 'Do you think you'll be able to carry them all, Billy? It'll be a bit heavy.'

'I'll be all right, Mrs Bramble.' He grinned. 'I'll cope.'

Ages ago he caught on to the idea that if he said he would manage the shopping with a struggle, but was only too glad to do it to help her out, she would give him sixpence instead of the usual three-penny piece. However, he felt slightly guilty about lying like that because the shopping was never that heavy and Mrs Bramble must be hard up.

Indeed, he knew she washed pots and things every night at the Spa Hotel down Buxton to help eke out the small pension she received from the quarry after her husband got killed. Hump once told him that when his mum came home late at night, which she always did, she sat in front of the fire and drank two bottles of Mackeson's Milk Stout, then cried and cried until she fell asleep,

'Every night?' Billy said.

'Well, nearly every night,' said Hump.

Again, as it had done before, Billy felt his heart go out to Mrs Bramble.

Mrs Bramble smiled, exposing her small, tobacco-stained teeth. 'Right, Billy,' she said and handed him a half-crown piece and the shopping list. 'It's all written down for you so you won't forget. I'll try and have Timothy ready to go out playing with you by the time you get back.'

'Right,' he said.

Mrs Bramble once more smiled fondly at him and reached forward and patted him on the head and ruffled his curls. 'What a good little boy you are, Billy,' she said; 'what a very bright little boy. Your mother should be very proud of you.'

Billy was too embarrassed to reply and scurried out.

When he got back from shopping Billy wasn't surprised to find Hump was still in his nightshirt and still sitting on his chair picking his nose. He was reading the Rover comic this time.

Billy saw two empty eggshells sitting in a twin eggcup on the plate on top of the three-legged stool placed by his side. It confirmed Hump had eaten his breakfast. There was also a crust of uneaten toast and a half-empty mug of tea by the side of it.

Mrs Bramble smiled and squinted at him through a cloud of tobacco smoke as she took the shopping off him. 'Timothy's not feeling very well,' she said, speaking past the cigarette in her mouth. 'He's not very strong, you know. His accident.'

'Oh,' Billy said though he knew Hump was as strong as an ox. He once saw him pick up a twenty-eight-pound coal weight and put it above his head, though it did wobble a bit.

Now he patiently waited while Mrs Bramble rummaged through

her purse. He was thrilled to see his reward was a bright, shiny sixpence. Mrs Bramble placed the coin in his hand and said warmly, 'There you are. Billy. Fair remuneration for a job well done. Now, did you make sure the cats hadn't been on the vegetables?'

Billy nodded vigorously. 'Oh, yes, Mrs Bramble.' But he didn't make sure. How could he ask Phyllis Forwards which vegetables escaped the attentions of her five cats? He got into enough trouble as it was without inviting it.

He turned and looked at Hump. 'See you later, pal?'

Hump nodded and grinned. 'Aye. This afternoon. Big Bushy?'

'Yeh.'

Meanwhile, Mrs Bramble looked fondly at Hump. 'Bless him,' she said. 'Don't you think he's a dear. Billy?'

Billy sniffed. He thought he was a mard arse at times. Hump leered at him over his comic.

'He's all right,' he said.

Out on the street again Billy raced down Leek Road, along Dolly Peg Row and skidded to a halt at Mrs Buyer's shop and composed himself. When he walked through the door the bell rang once and then rang again as he closed it behind him. Now standing at the long counter he said,

'Four Bull's Eyes and ten Woodbines for me dad.'

Mrs Buyer eyed him suspiciously. Billy became alarmed as she leaned forward over the counter and stared down at him through the gold-rimmed spectacles she wore on a gold chain about her neck. 'For your dad?' she said. She waggled a finger under his nose and added, 'I shall ask him, you know? Don't think I don't know what you're up to.'

Stunned, Billy stared back at her, hesitated for a moment, then turned tail and scurried out of the shop.

Outside on the pavement he paused to heap all sorts of calumny on Mrs Buyer, under his breath. The Old Bat was even smiling at him as he turned to close the door behind him. But the refusal now meant he would have to waste time going down to the Bottom Shop for cigarettes. They never asked there.

He hared off down the hill. He needed the fags. He needed to make some real pocket money out of this by selling the cigarettes on at a penny apiece to the gang, for he heard there was a good Tarzan picture on at the Spa Cinema next week and he didn't want to miss it.

When he got to the Bottom Shop, he hopped up the steps and went in. At the counter he said,

'Ten Woodbines, please.'

Mr Frost leaned over and looked down at him. 'I thought your dad smoked Player's Weights?'

Billy rubbed his nose. 'Well, he does, but he's decided to have a change.'

Mr Frost raised his brows. 'Oh, has he?'

'Yes,' said Billy and added, 'oh, and four Bull's Eyes for me.'

Mr Frost said, 'For running t' errand, I suppose?'

'Yes.'

Billy held his head down to hide his reddening face. He was never very good at lying. In fact his mum said she could read him like a book. But Mr Frost didn't seem to notice his embarrassment. If he did, he didn't let on.

Less than a minute later Mr Frost handed over the Woodbine cigarettes along with a white paper bag containing four Bull's Eyes.

'Five pence altogether. Billy,' he said, then warned, 'But don't you go smoking those cigarettes yourself, my lad. It's against the law. I don't want P.C. Hastings breathing down my neck if he sees you.'

'Oh, no,' Billy said, shaking his head vigorously. 'They're definitely for me dad.'

'Right, then,' said Mr Frost.

Billy closed the shop door behind him.

Outside on the step he breathed a sigh of relief. He popped a Bull's Eye into his mouth and then raced up Duke Street, up Holmfield Road, past the Recreation Ground and up into Grin Wood, hoping, when he got to Big Bushy, the gang would have a brew ready and would be wanting to know if he'd got any cigarettes.

But all the time he ran his cash machine of a brain was calculating. By selling his fags at a penny each, and not having one himself, he would make a profit of four pence – enough to pay for a seat in the front stalls at the Spa Cinema.

The Famous Footballer's cigarette card in the packet he would give to Wesley to put in his latest album. They both got a lot of pleasure looking through them in winter.

CHAPTER THREE

MEDICINE

It was near the end of May and Billy was sitting on the long brown bench placed hard against the vestry wall of the Chapel. He wasn't in a happy mood. He was studying the polished brown knots standing slightly proud of the plain pine boards that made up the vestry floor.

Why was he here? That's what he wanted to know. He always went to Church with his granddad on a Sunday morning to sing in the choir, but instead his dad dragged him here to the Chapel.

He stared at his father, who was sitting on the chair near the organ pump handle. His face was even more rubicund than usual He heard his mother call him a 'drunken sot' when he came home late last night. She also told him to 'bugger off and never come back, if that's all he could do.' But what shocked Billy most of all was the fact that his mother swore. He'd never heard her swear before. She always said beggar off when she really meant bugger off, which, apparently, made it all right. He made a mental note of the fact that his mother did swear last night. It might come in useful when he inadvertently swore and his mother wanted to use her dolly stick on him – if she could catch him, that is. But his dad looked really poorly this morning. He was leaning forward holding his head between his hands while shaking it.

'Never again. Billy lad,' he said.

Billy frowned. 'Never again what, dad?'

His father looked at him, his eyes bloodshot 'You wouldn't understand if I told thee, lad.'

Pulling a face Billy leaned back and rested his shoulders against

the wall behind him and stared at the wall opposite. Like all the other walls in the room it was painted green and cream, the colours separated by a black line. On the wall across from him was a row of brass coat hangers. They were fastened to a brown painted chamfered board, which was secured to the wall with screws. Coats and hats were hanging from the hooks.

Out of habit Billy made to wipe his nose on his coat sleeve, but restrained himself at the last split second when he remembered he was wearing his Sunday Suit. His Sunday Suit was special. It was bought solely for him. Oversize, of course, but his. His mum explained to him one day, when he complained it was too big, that she needed to buy a larger size so he could grow into it and she could get the most for her money, because money didn't grow on trees.

At the time he did look round to see if money did grow on some trees, but he found, in the end, his mother was right

However, because money was so scarce, the rest of his clothes were usually other people's cast offs. Some of his clothes were things his brother Luke had grown out of. Luke was five years older than he was and, as a consequence, the cut-down clothes still hung on him like rags on a scarecrow, even though his mum did do her best to make them fit. And he knew the need for frugality didn't end there. When clothes were finally declared beyond repair they were usually cut into strips to make peg rugs with to save wear and tear on the lino.

The recollection of peg rugs caused warmth to fill him for a moment. He liked nothing better than to sit in front of a glowing coal fire on a cold winter's evening helping his mum and his granddad and sister to make peg rugs.

He looked round the vestry. He yawned, hugely. Having little sleep last night, because his parents' rowing, was now beginning to take its toll. And having to sleep with all the family in the big attic at the top of the three-storey cottage they lived in didn't help matters either,

But topping it all, having his dad insist a candle be kept lighted all night so he could use it to see his way down the two flights of stairs to reach the toilet outside at the back made matters even worse. He heard him tell his mum, in a slurred voice, he needed to keep a light on because he had the runs and he thought it unreasonable to use the chamber pot because of the smell it would cause. Billy thought that was considerate of him but his mum just made an angry noise. And Billy knew the reason why they all slept in the attic was down to the fact that his Aunty Olive and his Uncle Fred and his two cousins, Jim and Doug, also lived in the cottage, They had the two rooms on the middle floor. They would normally be the two bedrooms in the cottage. One they used to sleep in, the other to eat and relax in. Aunty Olive and Uncle Fred even had a three-piece suite and a radio in their living room. His granddad, on the other hand – and Billy thought it unfair – was obliged to sleep on the couch on the ground floor living room, because there wasn't a room left for him upstairs.

That always made his granddad last to bed and first to rise.

Billy rubbed his nose pensively. Not that the crowded situation bothered him overmuch for he was hardly ever in the house. Morning and evening he did his newspaper round, in-between that, he went to school. If they wanted him at the sawmill, he did his stick-chopping-and-bundling job in the evening, after tea. Indeed, most of the time he just went home to eat and sleep; the rest of the time he played out with the gang. It was no hardship. He loved being out of doors.

He sagged against the vestry wall. He was relaxing deeply when the booming voice of Mr Goodfellow, the regular preacher at the Chapel, brought him upright and wide-awake again.

Mr Goodfellow, he realised, was announcing the number of the first hymn to be sung. Following his words came the sounds of people getting to their feet and coughing and rustling through hymn-books to find the right page from which to sing. The sudden movements brought a groan from his dad. He climbed wearily to his feet and began to work the handle, which, Billy knew, delivered air to the organ so it could be played.

Soon melody cascaded forth as Miss Bolthardy – who Billy knew was the organist as well as one of the teachers at school - fluttered elegant fingers over the keys before striking the chord that, Billy also appreciated being a choirboy, was hit to lead the congregation into joyous song. Billy soon found himself being carried along by the well-known tune and it wasn't long before he was singing in unison with the congregation.

His dad glowered across at him. 'Now don't thee start. It's bad enough having those out there going on without you putting your pen'orth in.'
A little hurt, Billy stared. 'Don't you like hymns, dad?'
'I've got a headache.'
'But, it's one of me favourite hymns.'
'Well, it isn't mine,' his father said, 'so shut it.'
Billy found himself sinking into a sulk. He knew his dad and granddad held different views on Religion, as they called it. His dad argued what he saw during the First World War cured him of any previous belief he might have held of a Being that was benevolent and caring. His granddad, on the other hand, definitely held the opposite view. He said his wartime experiences only helped to strengthen his Faith in the Lord. But sometimes their arguing got so heated his mum needed to step in and tell them to stop behaving like children.
'Roll on t' sermon. Billy lad,' his dad suddenly sighed, 'that's all I can say. I need me medicine.'
Billy eased up off the wall, his sulk forgotten. 'What sort of medicine?'
'Ind Cope's elixir, lad,' his dad said. He managed to flicker a grin. 'The hair of the dog, you might say.'
Billy frowned. He'd seen 'Ind Cope's Best Ales Sold Here' written above the door of the Duke of York pub, but it didn't say anything about it being medicine. As for the hair of the dog… what was that supposed to mean?
'Me mum's got some Indian Brandee in the cupboard at home,' he said, wanting to help because he really did like his dad.
His dad's grin, this time, flashed a glimpse of his white teeth, which he polished over the slop stone in the kitchen twice daily using solid dentifrice.
'Oh, nay, lad, that's not t' sort of medicine I'm on about,' he said. 'I want summat a bit stronger than that.'
Billy frowned 'Such as?'
His dad tapped the side of his nose. 'Never thee mind. And don't say owt about it to thee mum. Am I making myself clear?'
'No.'

'Well, just think on, lad,' his dad said, 'you're bright enough. I don't want her on at me again if she hears about it.'

'What?'

His dad let out an exasperated sigh. 'Just don't say *owt*, got it?'

'Yes.'

His dad went on pumping.

Billy went quiet, but was still puzzled.

After working the handle for a minute or so his dad waved his free hand and grinned at him. 'Come here, lad,' he said, 'I want to see if you can pump this organ.'

Billy reared up off the wall and got up. Was this what he was here for? When he took hold of the pump handle his dad closed his hand firmly over his. 'Now, lad,' he said, 'follow my rhythm. You'll soon get the hang of it.'

Billy found himself being jerked back and forth by his dad's pumping. It took him some moments to adjust his balance and get into the hang of it. When he did, his dad beamed down at him.

'Nowt to it, eh, lad?'

Billy grinned. 'No.'

His dad said, 'So you'll have no trouble doing it, then?'

'Eh?' Billy said.

Guarded caution reared up in him.

'The thing is, lad,' his dad said. 'I'll be wanting you to pump the organ. Now, I'm going to let go and leave you to it. However, before I do, I want to make one thing very clear: you must keep working the handle at all times. If you let go, just for a second, the organ will stop playing and we'll be trouble. Dost understand?'

'But,'Billy said,

His dad must have thought he said 'yes' because he said, 'Good.'

Billy found he was pumping alone. He began to work the handle furiously, but felt his dad's hand on his shoulder. 'Ease up, lad,' he said, 'you'll wear thee self out. Nice and steady, that's the ticket.'

Billy slowed his movements. When he did he found the pump handle wasn't so difficult to work. In fact, he discovered he was beginning to enjoy the experience. In a strange way, it gave him a sense of power. And that feeling triggered another, more malicious thought. If he were to stop pumping it would be chaos out there. He grinned at the notion.

'Nowt to it, eh, lad?' his dad said, misinterpreting his smile.

'No,' Billy said. But he felt a tinge of guilt.

He continued working the handle, all the time growing in confidence, until the singing in the chapel ended and the organ fell silent. Now the noises of the congregation coughing and shuffling came as they seated themselves.

When things were quiet Billy heard Mr Goodfellow announce the theme of his sermon. Then he began his address.

'You can stop pumping now lad,' his dad said.

Realising he was still pumping Billy let go of the handle and went to sit on the bench again. But it was with some trepidation that he watched his dad reach for his flat cap, hanging on one of the coat hooks on the wall. Then his dad crossed to stand in front of the small mirror fastened to the opposite wall. He began setting his cap at a rakish angle, and inspecting his gleaming smile. But what intrigued Billy most, his dad seemed to have forgotten all about his headache. He was whistling and humming and when he turned to him he was grinning.

'Right, lad,' he said, 'I'm off now.'

Billy felt slight alarm. 'Where are you going?'

'For me medicine, lad; I told you.'

'But, what about the organ?' Billy said.

His dad was now pulling on his best jacket, over his canvas braces and white shirt. 'You can manage 'til I get back, can't you?'

'What if I get tired?' Billy said.

'You managed well enough just now, didn't you?'

'Yes, but you were there. If you're not, I might not be able to manage as well.'

His dad rubbed his bristly chin thoughtfully. 'Look, if I'm not back – only if mind – and you have to start pumping... there'll be a silver joey in it for you when I get back, if you keep it up. How does that sound?'

'Three pence?' Billy said.

Instantly, the world seemed a brighter place.

'Yes. That'll do thee, won't it?'

'Hey, yeh.'

'Good,' his dad said, smiling. 'I'll be off, then.'

Billy watched him go out through the open vestry door and into the brilliant sunlight. As silence descended – apart from the subdued noise beyond the vestry of Mr Goodfellow delivering his sermon – he began wondering what he'd let himself in for.

He stared at the motes of dust floating across the beams of sunlight streaming in through the tall opaque windows opposite. It was really hot.

He wiped the pimples of sweat off his brow and watched a bumblebee wander in through the open door. After buzzing about awhile, as though lost, it began trying to bash its brains out against the window opposite. Drowsily, Billy watched it, finding its buzzing in some way relaxing. He was so tired. He lay down on the bench…

He sat bolt upright. Mr Goodfellow's sonorous voice, he realised, was announcing the next hymn. Panic filled him. He swung his legs off the bench and stood up and looked drowsily round,

His dad was nowhere in sight.

He dashed to the door of the vestry and looked down the tarmacadam covered path to the wrought-iron gates that led out on to Macclesfield Road. There was no sign of his father. Alarming him even more, he heard throats being cleared and people shuffling to their feet in readiness to sing the next hymn. Causing more anxiety, he heard the sound of Miss Bolthardy's voice come from the trumpet-shaped end of a brass tube sticking out of the wall near the pump handle.

'Simon, begin pumping.'

His dad's name was Simon!

Galvanized, Billy ran to the handle. He began working it furiously. Soon, the organ trilled into life and after another rousing introduction, the congregation burst into glorious song.

After what seemed to be no time at all, and much to his chagrin, Billy felt his pumping arm beginning to ache. Anxiously, he changed hands. After a minute or so, he changed hands again. But strive as he might, the tones of the organ begin to sag and rise as his strokes got less regular. Something even greater than panic began to cause a tumult of anxieties to cascade through him.

'Oh, heck!' he moaned. 'Oh, heck!'

It was then Mr Parks, who lived down Macclesfield Road, came bursting into the vestry and brusquely took command of the handle.

'Ok, Billy, I'll deal with it,' he said.

Soon his vigorous, confident strokes caused the organ tones to even out. It was then Mr Parks frowned down at him.

'Where's your dad. Billy?'

'Gone for his medicine.'

'Medicine?' Mr Parks frowned. 'What sort of medicine?'

Billy shook his head anxiously. 'He didn't say. He said he'd be back. He said he wasn't feeling very good and needed his medicine.'

Mr Parks began rubbing his smooth chin with his free hand and saying 'hum.' At length he said, 'Well I think we all know what sort of medicine your dad's talking about, Billy.'

Billy gawped at him. 'I don't. He didn't tell me.'

Mr Parks looked kindly at him, 'No, perhaps not, lad.' He reached out with his free hand and patted him on the shoulder. 'I think you'd better get off home and leave this to me, son.'

'But, I promised me dad I'd pump,' Billy said. There was also the matter of three pence reward for doing a good job.

'Don't you worry your head about that, lad,' Mr Parks was saying, 'I'll have a word with your dad when he gets back from taking his medicine as he calls it. Also, I'm sure Mr Goodfellow will want a word with him, too.'

'But, I promised I'd–'

'And you did the best you could, lad,' Mr Parks said. 'Now, off you go; I'll square it with your dad. Don't fret.'

Billy trailed through the open door.

When he got home he closed the front door behind him, wanting to shut out such an unfair world. He sat down on the settee. The smells of beef roasting and cabbage and potatoes cooking filled the air. Presently, his mum came bustling in from the kitchen. She was wiping her hands on her apron. Her cheeks, he saw, were flushed.

Muttering, she opened the front door again and glared at him.

'What d' you want to do that for? Shut the door? It's like an oven in here.' Then she looked at him more closely. 'What's the matter with you? And where's your dad?'

'He's gone for his medicine,' Billy said glumly.

Instantly, his mum stiffened and her slim fingers clenched into fists by her sides until they trembled.

'I'll swing for him!' she said. She went back into the kitchen muttering weakly, almost unhappily, 'I will, I'll swing for him.'

Not knowing what 'swing for him' meant exactly, Billy thrust his hands down between his scarred, bare knees showing through his short trousers and stared miserably at the big rice pudding that was keeping warm on the open range hob.

His granddad came in through the door. 'Now, lad,' he said, 'You look like you've lost a shilling and found sixpence.'

Billy could only mumble as he watched his granddad take off his jacket and trilby hat and hang them up on the hook behind the front door. When he was settled in his armchair he said;

'Where's your dad, then?'

'Having his medicine.'

His granddad raised his grey eyebrows and then cleared his throat. 'Oh, I see. It's like that, is it?'

'Like what?'

'Nothing to concern you, lad,' his granddad said. He picked up The People newspaper off the small table beside his armchair.

Billy was about to pour out the full story to him... about pumping the organ, Mr Parks' intervention... when his mum came bustling in from the kitchen.

'He's at it again, father,' she said.

Billy gazed into her face, She'd clearly been weeping. And now he saw her lips begin to tremble once more. It always upset him terribly to see his mother cry.

'I know, lass,' his granddad was saying. 'But he saw some rum things in that war – at Ypres and on the Somme. It drove some men mad. It seems he just needs something to loosen him up now and again.'

'Other men were in the war,' his mother said bitterly, clearly forgetting her tears, 'they don't go boozing all the time.'

'That's a bit unfair, lass,' his granddad said. 'He hasn't touched for months as well you know. Summat must have triggered him off. You know what he's like.' He patted her arm gently, 'Leave it to me,' he added comfortingly. I'll have a quiet word with him.'

His mum sighed and said, 'I wish you would. Nothing I say seems to have any effect on him.'

'Don't run yourself down, lass,' his granddad said firmly. 'He's not drinking as much as he used to do so you must be getting through to him somewhere. Another good thing, he's never violent with it so that's something.'

His mum muttered and went back into the kitchen.

Billy picked his nose and then he took up the *Wizard* comic he swapped Wesley the *Rover* for and began to read what Wilson was doing.

But where was Ypres?

CHAPTER FOUR

JERUSALEM'S CUCKOO

It was the middle of June. It was nine o'clock on a bright Saturday morning. Billy was standing on Dolly Peg Row, opposite the school playground. His newspaper round was finished and his breakfast of bacon, egg, oatcake and tinned tomato was digesting nicely in his tummy.

He was gawping up at Wesley Ward, who was grinning down at him. Wesley was sitting on an old motorbike seat that was fixed to an iron frame and bolted on to the front of the flatbed cart he was atop of. A donkey was standing drowsily in the shafts. Wesley was wearing one of his dad's cast-off weskits, plus one of his dad's discarded flat caps, out of which stuck a long, white goose feather. Billy observed the cap was so over-sized the edges were hanging down over Wesley's jug-handle ears.

Not attempting to hide his amazement at the sight of the donkey and cart Billy said, 'Hey up, mate, where've you got that lot from?'

Wesley stuck his chest out. 'They've been left to me.'

'Gerrout,' Billy said.

He stared in wonder at the dusty, silver-grey donkey standing in harness between the bare ash shafts, the paint on which had long since been weathered off. The beast's eyes, Billy observed, were big dark pools, staring vacuously at a point directly ahead of it. Wesley beamed down at him.

'Well, what d' you think?' he said.

Billy screwed up his face to express his doubt, for Wesley could sometimes embroider the truth a little.

'Are they *really yours*?' he said

Wesley scowled. 'Course they're mine – I told you.'

'Who's left them to thee?' said Billy.

'Me great uncle Elijah,' said Wesley. 'He always said he would and he did.'

Billy nodded his head approvingly at the mention of Wesley's great uncle Elijah and said, 'Oh, aye, he were always all right were your great uncle Elijah.'

'There were nobody better, pal,' Wesley said proudly.

And with that further endorsement of great uncle Elijah memories began to flood through Billy. When he was living Wesley's great uncle Elijah was a tall, grey-bearded man who, more often than not, wore a big brown trilby hat and a black serge suit, which was often stained with food and, occasionally, cow muck. Other notable features about great uncle Elijah, Billy recalled, were his long, crooked, yellow teeth and his dubbined hob-nailed boots that turned up at the front and squeaked on the pavement when he walked. Some said great uncle Elijah was a penny short of a shilling, but when Billy asked his granddad what he thought about the comment his granddad said, 'He's nowt of the sort. Billy lad. Elijah's just a bit eccentric, that's all.'

Though not knowing what 'eccentric' meant. Billy knew about great uncle Elijah. When he was alive he lived in his rundown ten-acre smallholding on top of a hill on Brandside. The back of the farmhouse overlooked a deep, narrow gully that was filled with bilberry bushes, the fruit of which Wesley and he picked during the summer holidays so their mums could make pies out of them,

Great uncle Elijah, when he wasn't working part-time at Hillhead Quarry track-laying, looked after the farm, along with Wesley's great aunt Gertrude – until she died, that is. Billy recalled they milked three cows and owned a horse called Dragon, which they used for carting manure to spread on the fields in Spring as well as for pulling the rusty hay mower and the hay cart when the hay was dry and ready to stack in the barn. But some people said because it was so high up at great uncle Elijah's farm, he usually needed to shake the frost off the hay before he could get it in. Billy thought that a bit daft until he saw great uncle Elijah doing it.

Great uncle Elijah also owned a two-wheeled buggy, which he occasionally hitched the donkey to so he could take great aunt Gertrude for rides out. He would take her to Leek Market on a Wednesday and Buxton Market on a Saturday, regular as clockwork. When they were at the Buxton Market they could often be seen sitting outside the New Inn pub on the Market Place, smoking clay pipes filled with twist and drinking pints of Robinson's Best Bitter.

In the summer great uncle Elijah – being a kindly chap – used to hang the cage with his two budgerigars in outside the faded red front door of the farm, so they could sing and curse all day, like he taught them to, or so he once told Billy with a grin. He also owned two peacocks, six pigs and three goats. But when great aunt Gertrude died, great uncle Elijah got lax – or so Wesley's dad said. He started allowing his ten Rhode Island Red hens and the cockerel that went with them to wander into the kitchen. They would perch on the table and peck at the bread or eat whatever else was handy. And he didn't clean up after them much. Billy was always very careful where he sat and what he ate when great uncle Elijah invited him into the kitchen when he was visiting with Wesley. Wesley's mother definitely didn't approve of such goings on. She said it was very unhealthy and somebody should tell great uncle Elijah it was – not that it would make any difference, she added. He had always been of dubious habits had great uncle Elijah.

However, the very best thing about Wesley's great uncle Elijah, Billy now decided, was his Indian motorbike. It was a brute of a thing with great big swept back handlebars. It smelled of oil and petrol and when great uncle Elijah kick-started it up and twisted the throttle grip it blew out great clouds of blue smoke from the rusty exhaust pipe at the back and banged and popped and rattled like an old tin can filled with stones until the firing smoothed out and became regular.

Billy pictured great uncle Elijah now – a wild look in his eyes, his flat cap placed back to front on his head and secured by using the elastic of his airman's goggles. Dressed in that fashion great uncle Elijah would race round the back roads between Longnor and Hartington, Reapsmoor and Leek, honking the rubber bulb of his horn and shouting at people to get out of the way or he would knock them out.

Sometimes he would take great aunt Gertrude with him. He would perch her on the pillion and she would shriek with delight as they careered along to back lanes – her long, black, grey-streaked hair flying out behind her, her arms clasped tightly about great uncle Elijah's waist, her severe black frock flapping about her knees and showing her frilly white petticoats and black woollen stockings.

'Has t' gone to sleep?' Wesley said, frowning down at him.

Billy snapped out of his thoughts and grinned up at his pal. 'I were thinking about your great uncle Elijah,' he said.

'Oh, aye,' Wesley said, and then he sighed. 'Well, we won't be going up there any more, will we? It's up for sale. But me dad said we'll have to near give it away, because nobody wants to live up there. It's the arse end of nowhere.'

'I'd live up there,' Billy said.

'So would I,' said Wesley, 'but me dad said I've only seen it when it's been pleasant. He said wait until there is twenty foot snow drifts on t' ground, then go and have a look at it. What does he mean by that, pal?'

'I don't know,' Billy said. 'It would be all right for me. I like snow.'

But not really all that interested in the subject he screwed up his eyes and waved a hand at the donkey standing placidly in the shafts. 'So, where are you going to keep it now you've got it?'

'Down Ann Croft,' Wesley said, 'in one of them fields that run alongside t' Ochre Brook. Me dad's fixed it up with whatshisname – him who owns t' land. He's paying him so much rent a week for graze. But me dad said the beast had better earn its keep, or else out it'll have to go.'

Billy frowned, 'How can he sell it if it's yours?'

'That's what I've been wondering,' said Wesley. But seeming not to care too much he waved his makeshift whip. 'Anyway, are t' coming?'

'Where?' Billy said.

'This job I'm on,' said Wesley.

Instant delight filled Billy. 'Hey, yeh,' he said.

He hand-vaulted up on to the cart and sat down on the front edge of it, near the motorbike seat Wesley was sitting on. He allowed his legs to dangle into space. Settled in his seat, Billy looked along the donkey's dusty back. There was a dark, hairy cross on it – partly hidden by the worn harness. He'd seen such oddities on other donkeys and was always intrigued by them.

'What's that mark, Wesley?' he said. 'That cross thing on its back?'

'All donkeys have them,' Wesley said, sticking a thumb into one of the pockets of his dad's worn weskit. 'Me dad says it's there because Jesus sat on a donkey when he entered – er – what d'you call it…?'

'Jerusalem?' Billy said,

'Aye, that's the place,' said Wesley. 'It's summat to do with the Lord blessing the beast for carrying him over all them palm leaves they put down, though I don't know how me dad knows that – he never goes to church.'

'It's called Palm Sunday,' Billy said.

Wesley sniffed. 'Aye, well, I thought you'd know.'

Though Wesley sounded a bit scornful regarding his knowledge of biblical events, Billy decided to ignore it. It pleased him to know about such things, particularly the one about Jesus Entering Jerusalem On A Donkey. Indeed, he still liked to look at the picture of the event in the huge, leather-bound, illustrated family Bible his granddad kept on top of the cabinet, next to his armchair

But there were other features in the Family Bible that intrigued him. Such as the family's births, deaths and marriages, which were carefully recorded in fine script on the blank pages in the back of the Holy Book. The first entry was a birth. May the 4th 1792; the last was a death entered March the 6th 1875. There the entries ceased because the blank pages were full. Billy occasionally wondered where they wrote such family history now? However, he did know his granddad regularly read passages from the Good Book, as he called it, especially at night before he went to sleep on the settee. Once, when he asked his granddad why he read from the Good Book so much, his granddad replied it was because the Lord's hand had protected him when he was fighting the Germans in the Trenches in France during the Big War of 1914-1918. Then, tweaking the ends of his military moustache, his granddad would finish off by saying, 'Doing your duty by the Almighty, lad, is very important, and you'd do well to remember that.' Then granddad would cough and sniff and mop away the matter seeping out of the socket his glass eye was set in. Billy knew all about granddad's glass eye. Shrapnel had taken out his proper eye during the Big Push of 1916 on the Somme. It also left a big white scar along the left side of his head. No hair would grow on it. Billy was very proud of his granddad's war wound.

Wesley interrupted his thoughts again. 'We'd better be off,' he said. 'I don't want to be late, it's me first job.' He shook the reins suggestively and looked down. 'Are t' holding on, pal?'

'Aye, go on,' Billy said. 'Let her go.' He found excitement was now tingling vibrantly through him.

With a grin Wesley waved the whip in his hand. At best it was a piece of thick twine, attached to a willow switch. Wesley snapped the knotted end near the donkey's enormously long right ear but it was so ineffective the beast didn't even wiggle the member as the whip cracked above it. So Wesley shouted loudly, 'Gerrup, you owd sod!'

To Billy's surprise the beast obediently walked forward, adopting a sedate, head-nodding gait. It caused a degree of disappointment to well up in him. This wasn't how donkeys were supposed to behave. He'd heard donkeys were cantankerous beasts – as stubborn as anything on four legs. Already being intensely interested in the beast, he now felt the urge to point this out to Wesley.

His pal nodded, sagely. 'Oh, aye,' he said, 'it's true enough. You've just got to know how to handle them, that's all.'

To reinforce his point Wesley spat, with great emphasis, over the side of the cart. After waiting some moments for further explanation but not getting it. Billy said, 'So, how do you get them to move when they won't go?'

'Oh, there's plenty of ways,' Wesley said. 'Me great uncle Elijah used to use a stick with a spike on the end of it. When t' owd bugger got awkward he would jab its arse with it.'

'Did it work?' Billy said,
'Not very often,' Wesley said.
'Have you tried it?'
Wesley raised his eyebrows. 'Oh, aye.'
'What happened?'
Wesley sniffed and waggled his whip. 'The owd bugger started kicking hell out of the front of the cart, so I had to stop.'
'And that were it?' Billy said.
Wesley looked surprised. 'Oh, no, I've tried other ways.' He leaned over and picked up the very long stick with a carrot dangling from the end of it, which was lying alongside him on the bottom of the cart, near the frame securing the motorbike seat. 'I saw this in a comic once.'
'Oh, I've seen that in the Beano,' Billy said. 'Does it work?'
'It hasn't done up to now,' said Wesley, a little despondently.
Exasperated now by Wesley's lack of concrete proof that the methods he were explaining worked, Billy said,
'So, what do you do to get it moving when it doesn't want to go?'
'Whale the bugger with this,' Wesley said.
He waved his flimsy, makeshift whip.
Billy screwed up his face in disgust at another sighting of the puny lash. 'That?' he said. 'It wouldn't split a fart, that wouldn't.'
Wesley looked at him indignantly. 'It's better than nowt.'
Billy went quiet for a few moments and listened to the clip-clop of the donkey's hooves. Then he said, 'What does it do if a motor comes along?'
Wesley sniffed. 'It depends on how noisy it is. But there's not many motors about, is there? So it doesn't really come up, does it?'
'Say a lorry goes past,' Billy said. 'Summat noisy like a Derbyshire Stone wagon, what then?'
Wesley shrugged. 'I don't know because it hasn't happened yet, not with me anyway. I haven't had it long enough.'
Billy lapsed into silence once more until another thing that was intriguing him demanded explanation.
'Why do they have such big ears, Wesley?' he said.
His pal frowned. It was clear he was getting more than a little

annoyed with his constant probing, 'How the heck should I know?'

Billy shrugged. 'I just thought you might have asked your great uncle Elijah, that's all. You always say he knew all about donkeys and stuff.'

Wesley frowned. 'Well, I didn't,' he said. 'I'm not like you, you know – always asking questions.'

'Well, there's nowt wrong with that,' Billy said. 'As a matter of fact, me granddad says I should always ask questions. He said if I don't ask the questions I'll never get to know owt.'

'Your granddad's always saying summat according to thee,' Wesley said. Once again he spat over the edge of the cart, apparently this time with disgust.

'You've seen your backside this morning,' Billy said, feeling hurt by Wesley's unusual shortness of temper.

Wesley seemed to relent. 'Aye, well, wouldn't you have if your mum didn't give you any breakfast this morning?'

'What have you been doing?' Billy said.

'Nowt,' Wesley said. 'I only bust t' teapot.'

'That's enough, isn't it?'

'There were grease on the handle,' said Wesley indignantly. 'It slipped out of me hand. I nearly said she should have washed it properly, but I didn't want a clatter round the ear hole as well as having no breakfast.'

Billy went silent as Wesley turned the donkey off Dolly Peg Row and headed it towards Buxton, via Macclesfield Road. When they were going along Burlington Place, he said,

'So, what's this job we're going on, Wesley?'

'Moving an armchair and a sofa for Mrs Berwick to her daughter's house on Bridge Street, down Buxton,' Wesley said.

'How long will that take, d' you reckon?' Billy said.

'Haven't the foggiest,' Wesley said, and then frowned, 'Why?'

Billy hunched his shoulders. 'I just wondered, that's all.'

But he wasn't wondering, really. It was all about pocket money. He did Mrs Bramble's shopping on a Saturday morning. Indeed, he couldn't afford to miss doing her shopping for the reward he earned was all he got to spend on himself, but he didn't want to miss this trip with Wesley on his donkey and cart, either. He decided he must try and contact Mrs Bramble as soon as possible, to arrange to do her shopping this afternoon. He would have to settle for that, for he didn't want to miss this golden opportunity.

He was staring at the road passing under the cart when he realised the steady clip-clop of the donkey's hooves was no longer beating out its rhythm on the tarmac. Mystified as to why he looked up. He was surprised to see the beast was paused outside the Duke of York pub. It was staring down at Sammy Barton's ginger-haired mongrel. The dog was peeing against the pub's newly lime washed wall. Wesley, Billy realised, was already reacting to the situation because he was on his feet and whacking the beast's backside with the flimsy stock of his homemade whip.

'Gerrup,' he was shouting, 'it's only Sammy Barton's dog!'

But Wesley's pleas didn't seem to be having any effect on the donkey. It continued to stare fixedly at the mongrel, as if hypnotised. When the dog did turn round to see the donkey towering over it, it immediately bristled and began to bounce forward on stiff front legs, barking furiously and baring its yellow fangs.

Instantly, the donkey's tail and ears shot up. Then the beast wheeled about, dragging the cart round with it and went charging up the road. Before he hardly realised it. Billy saw they were passing Burlington Place and that the two buxom ladies who were busy donkey stoning their front steps when they went past them earlier, were standing and staring open-mouthed as they went careering past.

It was about this time that Billy became aware Wesley was swearing like a trooper as he tried to bring the bolting donkey to full order. Also, Billy now appreciated the cart was swaying violently he was in imminent danger of being thrown off it.

In desperation he lunged to his right and grabbed hold of the rusty frame supporting the motorbike seat Wesley vacated moments ago. Securing a firm hold on it he anxiously hung on, trying to stay aboard as the stampeding, braying donkey gathered momentum and the yapping, puny dog got left far behind.

Now, all was a blur to Billy. Cart, donkey, Wesley and himself were charging past the War Memorial, then the School House, then

Bonsall's Corner, then Constable Hastings' cottage, then Burbage Garage. Soon, Billy realised, they were rushing past the end of Holmfield Road before rattling up the tarmacadam Leek Road toward Canholes and Ladmanlow.

It seemed an eternity passed before the cart finally came to a halt. When it did. Billy lay panting and bruised on the worn boards. His arms were aching; his fingers and palms were rubbed red raw from grasping the rusty metal of the seat frame. What was even more disconcerting, he realised his heart was still thumping madly against his battered ribs,

He waited for it to calm down and then tentatively released his grip on the seat support and looked up. He saw they were stopped alongside the advertising hoardings Under Grin, known in the village as the Local Boards. It took some moments for him to appreciate the donkey was still braying shrilly.

'Can't you shut it up, mate?' he said.

Wesley, he observed, was standing stock still beside the motorbike seat. He was ramrod straight and staring fixedly ahead. His knuckles were white. He was still grasping the reins in a grip made clamp-like by the nightmare run. His dad's old flat cap was hanging down over his jug handle ears. Its tattered peak, Billy now saw, was also low enough to force Wesley to have to tilt his head back in order to see where he finally came to a stop.

At the sound of his voice, Wesley relaxed his grip on the reins and carefully adjusted his cap. Then he looked down. His disgust was plain, 'And how d' you propose I do that, clever bugger,' he said, 'put a bag over its head?'

Billy flapped his arms helplessly. 'Whatever. Anyway, didn't your great uncle Elijah tell you how to make it stop its noise?'

'No,' said Wesley,

With that curt reprimand Billy fumbled around in his mind for some idea that might work on the beast.

'Has it got a name?' he said, presently.

'Jerusalem's Cuckoo, if you must know.'

Billy couldn't believe it at first for it was the daftest name he had ever heard. He said,

'Did you say *Jerusalem's Cuckoo*?'

'Yes,' said Wesley. 'Wash your ears out.'

But Billy was already crumbling down on to the cart's worn boards. And his laughter was so loud it carried over the blue-slated roofs of the cottages Under Grin, showing above the level of Leek Road,

Wesley looked incredulous. 'What's so funny?'

'Jerusalem's Cuckoo!' chortled Billy. 'Who come up with a name like that?'

Wesley looked even more indignant. 'Me great uncle Elijah.'

'It couldn't have been anybody else,' Billy hooted.

However, Wesley continued to stare, as if not comprehending the ludicrousness of the name. Indeed, it was some moments before a slow smile began spread across his pixy-like features. Then he said, "Oh, aye.' He began to chuckle.'I never thought about it like that before because me great uncle Elijah reckoned it were t' best name he ever come up with. Took him a week to work it out.'

'I'm not surprised?' howled Billy.

Wesley began to crumble to the boards and Billy found he needed to move quickly to one side in order to allow his best pal to join him on the cart bottom. Then they both began to howl their amusement with great abandon.

It was some minutes before Billy managed to stop laughing. When he did and he became still, he stared into the blue sky and began to wonder what there was to laugh about after their very lucky escape not minutes ago when Jerusalem's Cuckoo decided to bolt. It was right curious. But perhaps his reaction to the donkey's name was a safety valve, after his and Wesley's recent encounter with real danger? His granddad said such things occurred occasionally.

He gathered himself and sat up. Then, on hands and knees, he made his way to the front of the cart. Sitting down on the edge he felt empty and slightly bewildered. He stared at the now silent donkey peering at him from beyond the worn shafts of the cart. The beast, he saw, was waggling its massive ears about as if it were trying to work out what was so funny.

Billy leaned over and nudged the still chortling Wesley, rolling about on the cart bottom.

'It's staring at us,' he said.

His pal slowly stopped laughing and gazed at him. 'What is?'

'Jerusalem's Cuckoo,' Billy said.

Wesley continued to stare at him. 'So what?' he said. 'It's always staring at summat. That's all the daft bugger ever does is stare.'

'I just thought you'd want to know, that's all,' Billy said.

Wesley had definitely seen his backside this morning.

'So you've told me,' snorted Wesley.

He slowly got to get to his feet. As he did, Burbage church clock began to strike ten and a look of alarm instantly came to his pixie features. 'Oh, heck,' he said, 'I promised Mrs Berwick I'd be at her daughters by ten o'clock to pick up that furniture. Me dad said I must look after me customers, or I soon wouldn't have any.'

Briskly, Wesley plonked himself down on the motorbike seat and stared down.

'Are you holding on, pal?'

'Yeh,' said Billy, anticipation again keen in him, 'let's get moving.'

Grinning, Wesley gathered up the reins. 'Right, see if owt's coming from behind, I want to turn round.'

Billy wished he hadn't looked because the first thing he saw was P C Hastings pedalling his bicycle furiously towards them, coming from the direction of Burbage. Billy's alarm grew rampant and he tugged at Wesley's leg.

'Hey up,' he hissed, 'Hastings is coming.'

Pure horror filled Wesley's gaze. 'Oh, heck,' he said, 'what does he want?'

'Us by t' looks of it,' Billy said.

'What have we done?' Wesley said.

P.C. Hastings was red-faced and puffing when he dismounted beside the cart and stared at them. 'Now, then,' he said, lifting his cleft square chin, his gaze severe, 'you two caused quite a stir in the village just now.'

'Did we?' Wesley said.

Billy said, 'Why, what have we done?'

P.C. Hastings looked at them sternly. 'We'll come to the offence in a minute. First, I want to know if you're all right?'

Wesley frowned. 'Why, shouldn't we be?'

'That donkey of yours bolted, didn't it, lad?' P.C. Hastings said.

Wesley shook his head. 'Oh, no, it weren't bolting, it were running.'

P.C. Hastings rubbed his chin, frowning. 'Is there a difference, lad? If there is, it's news to me.' Then he said, looking from one to the other, 'Now then, which one of you was driving?'

Wesley said, 'I was.' He couldn't very well say he wasn't with the flimsy whip in his hand,

'Are you competent, lad?' P.C. Hastings said, elevating his blond brows and looking very superior.

'What does competent mean?' Wesley said.

'It means do you know how to drive such vehicles in a safe and proper manner,' said the constable.

Wesley pushed out his chest. 'Oh, aye,' he said, 'I know all right. Me great uncle Elijah taught me how to handle donkeys and horses long ago. You couldn't tell me great uncle Elijah owt about horses and donkeys. He pulled the big guns up to the Front in the Great War with horses did me great uncle Elijah.'

'Elijah Ward who lived on Brandside and now deceased?' P.C. Hastings said, raising his eyebrows in an enquiring way.

'What does deceased mean?' Wesley said.

'Dead, lad.'

'Yes,' Wesley said.

Constable Hastings rubbed his chin. 'I see.' He appeared to go into deep thought before he said, with a sigh, 'Very well, I'll give you the benefit of the doubt this time?' Then he waved a thick finger. 'But, if it occurs again, I'll be having a word with your dad. Am I making myself clear?'

'What d' you want a word with him for?' Wesley said.

'Because we don't want donkeys and carts careering around the streets endangering life and limb, that's what for, lad,' said P.C. Hastings.

'Oh,' said Wesley.

Billy said, 'So, can we go now?'

P.C. Hastings stared at him. 'What's your hurry, William?'

'You've finished with us, haven't you?' Billy said.

P.C. Hasting formed what could be called a smile on his thick lips, but Billy thought it looked more like a snarl. 'Oh, no, lad,' the constable said, 'There's another much more serious matter I want to take up with you two.'

'Such as what?' Billy said.

'The use of bad language in a public place,' P.C. Hastings said.

'Who says we were swearing?' Wesley said.

'Witnesses at the scene, lad,' said P.C. Hastings, frowning severely.

'I only said bugger,' Wesley said, 'that's not swearing.'

'The complainants think it was, lad,' said Constable Hastings, 'and what's more, so does the law.'

'What does complainants mean?' Wesley said.

'The people who reported the incident, lad,' said P.C. Hastings, 'They complained. Don't they teach you anything at that school?'

Billy said, 'He only swore once.'

'Once is enough, lad,' said P.C. Hastings. 'We can't have people wilfully using profanity in public places.'

'What's profanity?' Billy said.

P.C. Hastings stared at him. 'Are you trying to be funny, William?' he said.

Billy shook his head vigorously. 'No.'

'Well, it means swearing, lad,' said P.C. Hastings,

'Oh,' said Billy and wondered why P C Hastings didn't say that in the first place.

P.C. Hastings stared at them without speaking for some moments. Then he said, 'Very well, I'm prepared to overlook the matter this time. But' – he wagged a severe finger and looked at them both, in turn – 'if I hear any more about that donkey bolting, or hear about the use of bad language on the streets, I'll come down on you like a ton of bricks. Is that clear?'

Wesley said, 'Yes.'

'William?' said P.C. Hastings.

'Yes,' Billy said.

Wesley, now clearly thinking they were dismissed, made to start turning the cart, but P.C. Hastings held up his hand. He even smiled, vaguely, 'Whoa, hang on a minute, lad,' he said, 'I haven't finished with you yet. There is another matter that has recently been brought to my attention. Ran Tanning – going through the village at night knocking on peoples' doors and then running away… disturbing the peace in other words. What d' you know about that?'

Billy immediately shook his head 'Nowt,' he said innocently.

Wesley said, with a virtuous look, 'We don't do Ran Tanning.'

'Perfect little angels are we?' said P.C. Hastings with some irony. He rubbed his cleft chin. 'We're not getting very far, are we? Well, just remember, I've got my eyes on you and I won't be so lenient the next time.'

The constable climbed on to his bicycle and pedalled off towards Ladmanlow. As Billy watched him go round the rocky bend in the road he said, 'Suppose he tells us parents?'

Wesley shrugged, 'He didn't say he would.' He nodded his head rearwards. 'Look what's coming, pal.'

Billy turned. 'All clear,' he said.

Wesley made himself comfortable on the motorbike seat and then snapped the whip near Jerusalem's Cuckoo's enormous right ear, then he bawled,

'Gerrup, you old bugger.'

They both hooted with laughter as they cantered down the road.

CHAPTER FIVE

JERUSALEM'S CUCKOO (2)

Burbage church clock chimed six times with sonorous tones. The warm, early morning air hissed through Billy's close-cropped wiry brown hair as he charged down the road on his way to do his newspaper round for Mr Belham. His mum's parting words – as he ran out through the open front doorway – were still ringing in his ears.

'It's Sunday don't forget. The choir? So come straight back for your breakfast. No going off anywhere.'

No fear of that, thought Billy. He loved his Sunday Breakfast and he didn't mind going to church to sing in the choir with his granddad. He liked his granddad, even though he did sometimes ask him to do jobs when he wanted to be out playing with the gang. There was also another thing he was pleased about – the job he was on yesterday with Wesley Ward and Jerusalem's Cuckoo. It went well; so well he was able to fit in Mrs Bramble's shopping, for which he received three pence for doing a good job. Also the business of being involved with P.C. Hastings now seemed a bad dream, better forgotten as soon as possible. Indeed, on this fine morning, his heart was singing with happiness. Only one thing marred this otherwise perfect day – the tortured braying coming from the vicinity of Ann Croft.

Billy knew it could only be the Cuckoo from Jerusalem.

When he reached Mr Belham's twelve by sixteen foot lock-up shop, which his employer called his 'business premises'. Billy was surprised to find Mr Belham was already there. He was opening the hemp-tied bungles of newspapers that were usually piled against the green painted door, awaiting their arrival. There was also another thing that Billy was amazed to see – his employer looking decidedly bothered. He was usually such a calm person was Mr Belham. However, this morning, a deep frown clouded his narrow brow, as he stood pale-faced and baggy-eyed behind the long, brown-painted five-ply counter they used to do their sorting on.

Mr Belham was shuffling – more like fidgeting – through the newspapers already strewn across the counter. He was puffing impatiently on the Park Drive cigarette dangling from his thin purple lips. And, as usual, the smoke from the cigarette was coiling up into his grey, watery eyes. The right eye, in particular. Billy noticed, was watering copiously and his employer occasionally dabbed it with his big white handkerchief, which he fished out of his black overcoat pocket.

And whenever Mr Belham smoked, he coughed. Short, chuffing coughs that seemed to bubble up from deep within his narrow chest Billy once asked his granddad why Mr Belham coughed so much. His granddad said it was because the Germans gassed Mr Belham when he was fighting them in France during the Great Conflict. But there was another reason, his granddad added – Mr Belham smoked too much. 'Moderation in all things, lad,' his granddad advised, 'that's the ticket to a long and happy life.'

But, snapping him out of his thoughts, Mr Belham said, 'Now then, Billy lad, are t' all right?'

'Yes,' Billy said, wanting to add, 'but you don't look very good.' However, he held it back,

'Good,' Mr Belham said and sniffed. 'I'm glad somebody is.'

He took out a bag of Mitcham's Mints from his overcoat pocket and popped a couple into his mouth. Billy knew he used them to relieve his cough, or was it his indigestion? He wasn't quite sure. Mr Belham also used Fisherman's Friends. Perhaps those were for his cough? Anyway, as usual, Mr Belham shook the bag under his nose and said, 'Here, take a couple, lad, seeing as you're partial to them.'

Billy took the peppermints and put them into his mouth before dutifully beginning to sort out his newspaper round. However, it was still obvious that Mr Belham was very upset about something. Maybe,

Billy pondered, it was because Joe 'Piggy' Piggott, the other newspaper delivery boy, hadn't arrived yet?

'Now then, lad,' Mr Belham said, 'you usually know what's going on about the village.'

He waggled a finger in the direction of Ann Croft. 'That donkey making all t' racket down there – whose is it, d' you know?'

'It's me mate's, Wesley Ward's,' Billy said, not attempting to hide his pride. 'It's called Jerusalem's Cuckoo. Wesley's great uncle Elijah left it to him when he died, along with a flat cart.'

Mr Belham raised his thick, greying eyebrows. 'Oh, did he now?'

'Yes,' said Billy, 'he's right chuffed about it is Wesley.'

'I can imagine,' his employer said, with some irony. He frowned. 'What is he intending to do with them? Has he told you, lad?'

'Cart stuff,' Billy said, 'so he can earn some money.'

At that piece of information, what could only be described as a conciliatory change came to Mr Belham's otherwise troubled features. 'Oh, I see,' he said. He sniffed and rubbed his chin. 'Well, I'm not against a bit of enterprise, lad – far from it – being a businessman myself. However' – he waved another irritated finger towards Ann Croft – 'having to put up with that racket every morning' – he sighed – 'well, I've got to say, it's going a bit far. And, what's more –'

Mr Belham stopped abruptly and began to cough. The attack was so violent the force of it flirted his cigarette straight out of his mouth. It shot like a glowing white dart across the room and hit the brown-painted street wall opposite amid a shower of sparks before it dropped to the floor. Then Mr Belham bent over his lanky frame and clasped his knees with his big, bony hands and began to cough in earnest. His thick red tongue stuck out like an enormous hen's and his face began to swell alarmingly and go a vivid purple as his convulsions grew. At one point Billy thought Mr Belham was going to be sick and it prompted his to ask, anxiously,

'Are t' all right, Mr Belham?'

His employer eased off long enough to look up and wave an arm to reassure him. 'Oh, aye,' he gasped, 'I'm all right, lad; it's that donkey that's upsetting the applecart. It's getting Mrs Belham into a right state I can tell you and, as a result, it's not doing me a lot of good, either. You see, Mrs Belham needs her sleep, lad, which she's not getting at the moment because of that danged animal's racket. Four o'clock this morning it started.' Mr Belham's face became gaunt-looking, even haunted. 'Why, it's enough to wake the dead,'

Billy, not able to find anything remotely helpful to say, and wondering how anything could possibly waken the dead, said, lamely, 'Oh, I see,' and set about assembling his newspaper round,

Eventually, Mr Belham ceased coughing and straightened up. Puffing wheezily, he tapped his chest.

'It's t' tubes, lad,' he said, 'they're jiggered. Gas, you know.'

'Aye, I know,' Billy said, 'me granddad told me.'

'Well he'd know,' said Mr Belham, 'he was there at the time was your granddad, but he had his gasmask on. He got me down the Line for treatment did your granddad. I tell you, lad, he probably saved my life.'

Billy folded the *Sunday Times* and added it to the growing pile in front of him. Then he thought, proudly: me granddad never mentioned that when he told me about Mr Belham getting gassed.

Mr Belham hawked up phlegm and crossed to the open door and spat a great glob of the matter across the pavement into the cobblestoned gutter close by. When he returned amazement was written all over his face. 'Whatever possessed Elijah to do it, lad,' he said, 'give young Wesley that donkey?'

Billy wiped his nose on his jersey sleeve, it was a habit he had when imparting important information. 'So he could cart things, like I said. He promised Wesley he would leave it to him and he did.'

Mr Belham 'harumphed' irritably and formed his large white handkerchief into a pad. He lifted his greasy black trilby hat and, with agitated gestures, began to mop away the beads of sweat stippling his pale baldpate. Replacing the handkerchief in his pocket he said, 'Well, I don't know what they're making of it down Ann Croft, lad, but I'll tell you one thing: it must be absolute bedlam down there. They mustn't have got any sleep at all last night with that racket.'

'Why not?' Billy said, frowning.

He'd slept like a log.

'Why not?' echoed Mr Belham. 'Because of t' noise, lad; that's why not.' He leaned forward, narrowing his eyelids. 'D' you know if anybody's had a word with Wesley's father about it?'

Billy shook his head. 'Not as far as I know.'

'Well, somebody should,' said Mr Belham firmly. 'If I catch him in the Duke of York this dinnertime I'll make a point of broaching the subject myself. One thing is for sure, we can't go on like this.'

Not knowing what 'broaching' meant Billy was on the point of asking when Joe 'Piggy' Piggott came in and Billy noticed straight away that Piggy smelt of cigarettes. And he immediately assumed that Piggy must have picked up a cast off dog-end from the gutter on the way to Mr Belham's lock-up, lighted it and smoked it before he came in. Piggy was always doing that. It never seemed to bother him that he might catch some horrible disease, like Billy's granddad warned him he would do when he caught him doing the same thing last back end.

'You're late, Joseph,' Mr Belham said sternly.

'T' alarm didn't go off,' Piggy said.

'Blaming that clock of yours again, lad?' Mr Belham said.

'Me dad said he's going to get a new one when he can afford it.' Piggy's rosy, porky face expressed the hope that would be sufficient explanation.

'Did he now?' Mr Belham said, clearly unimpressed. He tapped the counter top with a bony finger. 'Well, lad, you should know by now that folks like their newspapers on the table come breakfast time, especially on a Sunday.' He wagged a finger under Piggy's nose, 'If you keep this up I can guarantee there'll be precious few tips coming your way this Christmas. In fact, you might not have a job.' Mr Belham frowned down at Piggy. 'Am I making myself clear?'

Anxiety filled Piggy's round face. 'That's not fair,' he said. He pouted and added, 'I'm only late now and again. It's not my fault if t' clocks broke.'

'Not fair, eh?' Mr Belham said. 'Well, you'll soon find out that nowt's very fair in this world.' He waved a hand towards Doghole. 'Anyway, didn't that donkey's racket wake you up? You live near enough to it.'

Piggy looked blank. 'What donkey?'

'The one making all t' noise?' Mr Belham said.

Piggy raised his eyebrows. 'Oh, that,' he said. He shook his head vigorously. 'No, I heard nowt.'

Mr Belham shook his head, as if in amazement. 'Nay, I give up. Some folks just don't seem to bother one way or the other.'

He pulled out his bag of Mitcham's peppermints and shook it under Piggy's snout. He said, 'Here, you might as well have a couple of these seeing as Billy's had two. Then, for goodness sake, get on with making up your round and try to be a bit more punctual in future.'

Piggy took the sweets. 'I will, Mr Belham, honest,' he said,

After taking the peppermints and popping them into his month Piggy secretly smirked across at Billy. Piggy was always doing something like that when Mr Belham wasn't looking. His favourite trick was to put his thumbs in his ears and waggle his fingers and put his tongue out and shake it

Mr Belham was putting the bag of peppermints back into his pocket when he said, 'Right you two, I'm going out for a bit of fresh air. But don't think you'll be able to slack,' he warned, 'because I'll be looking at you through t' window.'

Billy watched him go through the door, watched him breath in deeply the clean fresh morning air. But he wasn't ready for Piggy when he leaned over the counter and said, grumpily,

'He's seen his arse this morning, hasn't he?'

'It's Wesley's donkey,' Billy said; 'it's kept him and Mrs Belham awake half the night.'

Piggy's porker face took on a look of indignation. 'Well, he's no need to take it out on me,' he said. As if for good measure, he stared out through the open doorway and blew a quiet raspberry in Mr Belham's direction before he started sorting out his newspaper round.

Billy followed his example, but without the raspberry. He was eager to get on so he could tell Wesley Ward all about Mr and Mrs Belham not getting any sleep because of Jerusalem's Cuckoo's awful braying.

He finished his newspaper round in record time.

When he got home he immediately sat down at the table under the front window and waited for his breakfast to come. As usual, his granddad was sitting in his armchair in the corner by the radio, reading from his big, illustrated Family Bible. His dad must be already walking out in Grin Woods, Billy decided, as he did most Sunday mornings now he'd lost his organ-pumping job at the Chapel. He hadn't been having his 'medicine' lately, either.

Soon his mum came bustling in from the kitchen. She placed his breakfast on the table in front of him and said, 'When you've got that down you go and change into your Best Clothes ready for church.'

'Right,' Billy said.

He began to wolf down his breakfast – the whole dinner plate full: egg, bacon, oatcake and tinned tomato, which he smothered with brown HP sauce. He finished the meal by mopping up the rich bacon fat, brown sauce and tomato juice with a thick slice of white Co-op bread. Then he went bounding upstairs to the attic bedroom to change into his Sunday Suit.

Reaching the bedroom he discovered his brother Luke was still fast asleep in the squeaky three-quarter bed they shared. But that wasn't unusual. Luke worked as a projectionist until eleven o'clock every night except Sunday at the Spa Cinema down Buxton. Mum said he earned his lie in, working hard like he did.

Now hardly able to contain his excitement. Billy took off his patched play clothes and laid them on the cane-back chair at the foot of the bed, and then put on his grey flannel Best Suit. It was a routine he went through every Sunday morning in preparation for going to church to sing in the choir with his granddad.

Dressed, he briskly galloped down the stairs and put on his Best Boots, which he polished last night with Cheery Blossom Black before he went to bed. He was just about to hurtle through the open front door when his mother's shout from the kitchen brought him to a slithering halt on the threshold.

'Where are you going?' she demanded.
'To see Wesley.'
'Well, don't you dare be late for church,' his mother ordered.
'I won't,' Billy said.
'Just see as you're not,' his mother said. 'And if you get those good

clothes dirty, you'll have me to deal with.'

'I won't,' said Billy. 'So can I go now?'

'Yes,' said his mother. 'But think on, lad.'

'*Yes*,' Billy said impatiently.

With that he bounded out through the door.

He found Wesley ambling down Duke Street just as the church clock was striking nine. When he told Wesley about Mr Belham's anger regarding the noise Jerusalem's Cuckoo was making his pal looked completely unimpressed by the news. He hitched up the rope halter he was carrying over his left shoulder. 'Well, that's nowt new,' he said, sniffing a dangling bead of mucus back up his nose. 'We've had half a dozen folk round the house complaining about that since Friday.'

'You never told me,' Billy said.

Wesley raised his thin brows. 'I didn't think you'd be interested.'

Billy leaned forward. 'So, what did you tell them?'

Wesley shrugged. 'I said nowt – me dad did all the talking. He more or less told them to bugger off. You know what me dad's like.'

'How did that go down?' Billy said.

Wesley raised his brows. 'Not very well and in the end me mum told me dad to stop losing his temper, stop swearing so much, and try to do summat about it. She said if he didn't she might start losing some of the customers she made dresses and things for. She told him most of her best clients lived down Doghole and up Macclesfield Old Road.

'What're clients?' Billy said.

'Folks me mum does work for, I suppose,' said Wesley. He grinned. 'I thought you'd know that, smart arse.'

Ignoring Wesley's jibe – he was always mocking his curiosity – Billy said, 'What did your dad say to that?'

'He said he would have to think about it.'

A hint of concern now touched Billy, because he liked Jerusalem's Cuckoo and liked going out on the cart with Wesley.

'He won't be getting rid of it, will he?' he said.

Something akin to amazement filled Wesley's face. 'How can he?' he said. 'The donkey's mine, and the cart. Even me mum said so. She said great uncle Elijah stipulated that very clearly in his will.'

Billy frowned. 'What does stipulated mean?'

Wesley, Billy decided, was coming out with some big words today. Perhaps it was because he was becoming a businessman.

'It means they belong to me, definite,' Wesley said.

Billy heaved a sigh of relief. 'Oh, that's all right then,' he said. 'For a minute there you had me worried.'

Wesley fumbled with the rope halter over his shoulder. 'Anyway, I'm on me way to Ann Croft to get Jerusalem's Cuckoo. I've got another job on – carting two armchairs and a cast-iron bed frame and a mattress to a place on West Road, down Buxton. How about coming?'

'Hey, yeh,' Billy said, but his excitement soon died. 'Oh, heck, I can't I promised me mum I'd be back at half past ten to go to church with me granddad.'

Wesley pulled a face. 'You can give church a miss for once, can't you?'

Billy shook his head firmly. 'No. I'm not letting me granddad down.'

'You won't be letting him down,' said Wesley.

'I will,' Billy said. 'Anyway I've got me Best Clothes on. If I get them mucked up, I'll really be in trouble.'

Billy watched, feeling decidedly rotten, as disappointment filled Wesley's pixie face. However, his best friend soon brightened up. 'Well,' he said, 'there's nothing to stop you walking down to Doghole with me, is there? You won't mess up your clothes doing that, will you? And you'll be back in plenty of time to go to church.'

Billy shrugged, 'Won't do any harm, I suppose.'

Wesley cuffed his arm, 'So, come on then.'

He set off at a run and Billy slid on his hobnails as he tried to get purchase and catch him up. By the time they reached Doghole they were both panting hard. Along with Wesley, Billy leaned on the drystone wall encompassing the big meadow that belonged to Ann Croft farm. The field made a picture, basking in the bright June sunlight. And among the cow-trodden grass he could see oxeye daises, buttercups and lady smocks – as well as lots of other flowers he didn't know the names of. There were also butterflies floating in lazy dancing flight over the blooms while occasionally alighting on them. He could see Common Blues and Red Admirals, Peacocks and Tortoiseshells in abundance. He lengthened his gaze. Now he observed Jerusalem's Cuckoo at the far end of the pasture, close to the gleaming white farmhouse, which he knew was recently limewashed. The beast, he saw, was grazing peacefully on the sweet young grass, its back towards them. Wesley cuffed his arm once more, challenge in his gaze. 'I'll race you across t' field,' he said,

'We've only just run down here,' protested Billy.

'That was a couple of minutes ago,' Wesley said and he was over the wall in one bound, the soles of his hobnail boots flashing in the sun, the grey flannel patches on the seat of his short brown corduroy trousers in discordant conflict with the gleams.

Billy scrambled after him. He avoided the moss crusted thickly on the wall. He also contrived to save messing up his polished Best Boots by swerving around the cowpats that were distributed amongst the grass and flowers, though there were no cows in the pasture at the moment,

By the time he reached the other side of the field he was within a pace or two of catching Wesley. However, something very odd struck him as he ran. Jerusalem's Cuckoo wasn't even bothering to turn to see what all the commotion was all about. And coming to a halt near the drystone wall that separated the field from Ann Croft Farm's vegetable patch, he said, nodding towards the donkey, 'Is it deaf?'

Wesley nodded and grinned. 'Oh, aye, just a bit. The guns did it in the Great War, so me great uncle Elijah said.'

Billy stared, '*Proper war guns?*'

'Oh, aye,' Wesley said, 'Jerusalem's Cuckoo was in France with me great uncle Elijah, when he was fighting the Germans. He got very attached to the beast did me great uncle Elijah, or so me mum said. Because, amongst other things, me great uncle Elijah used Jerusalem's Cuckoo to take food and ammunition up to the Front Line – when he wasn't on the horses helping to bring the big guns forward so the troops could blast the Germans to Kingdom Come. But when the war ended great uncle Elijah thought the beast would be going back to England with him, but some High Ups decided he would have to go for war surplus instead – along with loads of horses and other stuff.'

Billy frowned.

'What's war surplus?' he said.

'Stuff the army doesn't want any more,' Wesley said, with some authority. 'They had some French people round to the barracks to have a look at what they'd got. Great uncle Elijah got very upset about it, so me mum said, because he knew French people ate horses and snails and he thought they would eat Jerusalem's Cuckoo as well.'

Billy stared in disbelief. 'Eat horses – and snails?'

'And frogs legs,' Wesley added, 'That's why everybody calls them Froggies.'

'You're kidding me,' Billy said.

'I'm not,' said Wesley. 'Anyway, to get back to the story – to avoid Jerusalem's Cuckoo being sold to the French, great uncle Elijah asked his officer if he could buy the beast and the officer said he didn't see why not.'

'So he bought it?' said Billy.

'Yeh,' said Wesley, 'course he did – and at a knockdown price. However, getting back to Jerusalem's Cuckoo being deaf: I mean – look at his ears; they're like funnels. It's just asking for trouble being near big guns with them ears.'

Now looking very important – it must be because Wesley now considered himself to be a businessman – Billy watched his best friend pull a big carrot from the right pocket of his patched corduroy trousers. He turned to the donkey and waved the vegetable in the air and called, cheerfully, 'Come on you silly owd sod – look what I've got for thee.'

Billy watched as Jerusalem's Cuckoo gazed at the morsel with dark, placid eyes. Clearly it seemed to be deciding whether or not the tit-bit was worth moving for before it walked slowly towards Wesley, nodding his head to match its gait After a further examination of the delicacy Jerusalem's Cuckoo took a tentative bite out of it and started crunching it between his big yellow teeth.

Looking immensely pleased with himself, Wesley grinned over his shoulder and said, as he fed the last of the carrot to the beast, 'Me great uncle Elijah used to say he was just a big owd softy when it came to carrots. Give it a carrot, he said, and it'd do owt for thee.'

Billy said, 'Oh, yeh? So, how come the carrot on a stick routine you were on about yesterday didn't work?'

Wesley glared. 'Trust thee to think of summat like that. Maybe dangling a carrot is not the same as handing it one.' Then he added, with a grin, 'Do you fancy riding him back?'

Instant elation winged through Billy, 'Hey, yeh,' he said. But then his joy died as quickly as it ignited. 'Oh, heck, I can't. I've got me Best Suit on.'

'So what?' Wesley said. He leered. 'You're not scared, are you – like you said I was before you bottled me boil?'

Billy pushed out his chest. 'No, I'm not.'

'So, gerrup on it, then,' Wesley said. He began fitting the rope halter over the donkey's head.

Indecision bubbled in Billy. The need to preserve his Best Suit was strong. And there was also the threat of his mothers dolly stick descending on his backside should he dirty the garments. Nevertheless, he'd never ridden a donkey before, never ridden anything for that matter He decided Wesley's offer was too good to refuse.

'Watch this,' he said. He grabbed the donkey's mane and swung up on to its dusty back, and then beamed down at Wesley.

'How about that then, pal?' he said.

Wesley looked unimpressed. 'That's the easy bit,' he said. 'Let's see what you do when we get moving.'

'You do all right,' Billy pointed out

'That's because I've been at it some while,' Wesley said.

'There's nowt to it as far as I can see,' said Billy.

'Oh, aye?' said Wesley. 'We'll see about that in a minute.'

With the rope halter now fitted over the donkey's head Wesley tugged at it and shouted in the beast's left ear, 'Right, move your arse!'

To Billy's dismay, Jerusalem's Cuckoo immediately made it clear he had no intention of moving with Billy Nobstick sitting on his back.

Instead, the beast leaned backwards on its haunches and showed his teeth and resisted Wesley's heaving strongly. After some moments of tugging Wesley glared at the beast. 'Move,' he yelled.

But Jerusalem's Cuckoo remained adamant.

Presently Wesley looked up. 'Kick it, Billy,' he said.

Billy met his friend's stare with alarm, 'Not likely,' he said; 'it'll bolt.'

'Will it heck,' Wesley said.

'It did yesterday,' Billy said.

'That were different,' Wesley said, 'Sammy Barton's dog frightened it. Anyway, it weren't bolting, it were running.'

'Oh, aye?' Billy said.

'Smack it with your hand then,' said Wesley.

Billy decided to rock back and forth on the donkey's back. He did so and called, 'Hup! Hup! Hup! Gerrup!'

Wesley howled, 'That's no use!'

After some moments of frustrated glaring Wesley ran to the stack of bean sticks leaning against the drystone wall that protected the large vegetable garden along the side of the farmhouse from the livestock. He selected a stout rod and came running back with it. 'Now then,' he said, glaring at Jerusalem's Cuckoo with some ferocity, 'we'll soon see who's t' boss.'

Alarm scuttled through Billy. 'What're going to do?'

'Whale the bugger with this stick!' said Wesley, 'what dost think?' Without hesitation he brought the stick down on the animal's rump.

Instantly, Jerusalem's Cuckoo shrilled a bray and took off across the pasture, its tail and ears erect, its back legs kicking out like the loose ends of engine con-rods. In what seemed to be the winking of an eye Billy found himself bouncing about like a cork on a stormy sea.

He frantically grabbed the donkey's mane and hung on. He quickly came to realise he was already in acute agony for the donkey's broad backbone felt like the tops of a rough stonewall as his private parts impacted viciously against it.

'Oh, oh, oh!' he howled with each jolt.

But as if this wasn't bad enough he now saw he was heading straight for the Ochre Brook, the stream that formed the border between Ann Croft and the fields Under Grin. Something akin to terror filled him. The stream, he knew, was named well. The rounded stones in its bottom and the soil of its steep sides were caked with orange-yellow iron oxide deposits, washed out of the ores buried deep within the coal seams on Burbage Edge.

'Jump!' he shrieked to Jerusalem's Cuckoo while hauling frantically on the mane to try and turn the beast. But it didn't hear him, or didn't understand plain English. And at the edge of the brook, the donkey stopped dead in its tracks and Billy found himself hurtling helplessly through the air, arms flailing.

He hit the opposite bank with a jarring thud before toppling back into the brook. As the icy water washed over him it seemed to snatch all the breath from his body. Struggling madly, he regained his feet. Now standing dripping in the centre of the stream he glared up at Jerusalem's Cuckoo, who was standing on the bank's edge gazing placidly down at him.

He roared, 'You stupid beggar?'

It was then Billy realised he was holding a soggy clod, probably detached from the bank as he tried to prevent himself toppling back into the brook. With a howl of rage he hurled it at the beast, but missed it by at least a couple of yards.

Jerusalem's Cuckoo looked down at him with what could only be disdain before trotting off to graze nearby.

Shivering and miserable, Billy climbed out of the brook. Standing on the bank he looked down at his Best Sunday Suit. It was a terrible mess. Not only that his scrawny legs, best stockings and best hob-nailed boots were plastered with the orange-yellow filth. He found utter despair consuming him.

'What am I going to tell mum?' he moaned to anything that was listening.

Just then Wesley came running up. 'Are t' all right, pal?' he gasped.

Billy glared at him. 'Do I look all right?'

Wesley flapped his arms. 'Why didn't you jump off, before you went into the brook?' he said.

'I didn't get chance!' said Billy. He held his arms wide and looked down. 'Look at me clothes, Wesley. I can't go to church like this. And if me mum sees this lot, she'll kill me. I've got to get them washed somewhere.'

Wesley immediately grinned. 'Hey, that's an idea.'

He began pacing up and down the stream bank. After moments he stopped, turned and poked out a finger. 'You can wash them at our house,' he said. 'Me mum and dad are out for the day.' He waved a hand at the June sun, blazing down. 'They'll soon dry in this heat.'

"But they still won't be dry in time for me to go to church,' wailed Billy. 'I'll still be in trouble, choose what.'

Wesley shrugged. 'Well, you can't have it all ways, pal,' he said.

Billy glared, 'It's all your fault. If you hadn't hit the stupid beggar with that stick it wouldn't have run.'

'You said you wanted a ride,' Wesley said. 'I thought I was doing thee a favour.'

'Some favour!' Billy snorted. 'And it were your idea.'

Wesley looked a little sheepish. 'Sorry, pal.'

'Ugh!'

Billy began pacing up and down the bank. Each step caused squelching noises to come from his booted feet. However, when he was calm enough he said, 'D' you think it'll work, Wesley? Washing me clothes at your house?'

'Can't see why not,' Wesley said, instantly becoming brighter. 'But there is one snag, you'll have to wash your clothes in me dad's allotment shed. If me brother Herbert comes in and sees you washing them in t' slop stone he'll want to know what's going on. And he'll certainly tell me mum if he does see you. You know what he's like.' Wesley pensively tapped a finger on his chin, then added, 'I tell you what: you go to our garden shed. I'll get a bowl and some soap and bring them to you. You can get what water you want out of the water butt.'

Billy sighed. 'It's better than nowt, I suppose,' he said. He certainly felt better about the situation than he did a couple of minutes ago.

Feeling utterly miserable now, sitting here on the empty wooden beer crate in Wesley's dad's allotment shed, Billy listened to the church bells pealing their Bob Majors over the village. As he listened his glumness grew. He should be in the vestry now, changing into his cassock and surplice, preparing to sing in the choir with his granddad. Instead, he was sitting naked here in Wesley's dad's allotment shed.

He looked down at the white flesh of his body that hadn't been exposed to the sun – from his neck to his knees – then at his hands. They were still red and wrinkled from scrubbing his clothes with carbolic soap on the galvanised steel washboard Wesley bought with the bowl. However, there was one thing that did console him: his clothes were as clean as it was possible to get them. Nevertheless, they did have a crumpled look about them when he hung them to dry in the sun on the wall of the goat enclosure nearby. Also, there was still a strong yellow tinge to them. He could only hope his mum wouldn't notice, but he had his doubts.

He leaned back against the shed wall and closed his eyes and listened to the pealing of the bells.

Almost wistfully, he gazed through the gap of the partly open shed door. He could see Mr Ward's vegetables, wilting under the hot June sun. There were rows of cabbages, peas, beans and potatoes. There were beds of lettuce and lines of radishes, plus white turnips and swedes – all young and growing vigorously. He recalled, with some pride, how he helped his granddad to manure, dig and set his three allotments.

But it was boring sitting here. He listened to the flies buzzing around the pigsty behind the shed. He could hear Mr Ward's two pigs snuffling and grunting in the swill trough. They were like the two pigs his granddad kept up at Uncle Norman's farm. They were being fattened up for Christmas, After slaughter hams and flitches would be salted down on the stone benches in the cellar at home, tongues would be pickled in the pickle barrel and brawn would be made out of the head flesh. Nothing would be wasted but the grunt, his granddad always said.

Billy could hear Mr Ward's goats now – a Billy and a Nanny – occasionally nickering behind the five-foot drystone wall enclosure next to the pigsty.

Billy sighed and settled back against the shed wall. It was so peaceful he could easily go to sleep if he didn't have his washing to consider.

He woke with a start. He scrambled up. How long he had been asleep he didn't know. He stumbled across the tool-littered shed and stepped out through the hut doorway. He looked towards the goat enclosure. With relief he saw his clothes, placed there earlier, were still draped over the wall and, what's more, looked dry. But on further inspection, he realised his Best Sunday Jacket was missing.

Definitely worried now Billy ran to the paddock wall and briskly climbed and peered over the top of it. To his horror, he saw the goats were munching, with apparent relish, on his jacket

'Gerroff it!' he howled. His anger rampant, he scrambled on top of the wall. His sudden appearance clearly startled the goats. They immediately stepped back and stared up at him with their strange, mottled eyes. Without thought Billy launched himself down into the enclosure and grabbed for his coat.

'Give it here!' he yelled tugging at it angrily.

The goats immediately began to vigorously resist his attempts to retrieve his coat. And, making matters worse, the Billy goat lowered his head in a threatening manner. Made extremely indignant by that aggressive gesture Billy clouted it on the nose with his fist and yelled,

'Let go of my jacket!'

The beast reacted instantly by attempting to butt him and with a yelp Billy scrambled for the wall. However, he wasn't quick enough. As he attempted to climb the wall he felt the animal's head butting him – once, twice, three times on his bare backside. Instantly he howled, 'Ow, ow, ow!' Then went up the wall like a rat up a drainpipe and near flew over the top. Dropping on the other side he scampered some yards away from the wall before he felt it safe to turn and look back.

He was happy to see the Billy goat was on a tether, which only allowed it to stand on the wall top and glare at him but could come no further. The Nanny, he presumed, was still eating his jacket. It was then he realised there was more danger. The rest of his clothes were still on top of the enclosure wall.

He began running round the paddock, dragging his trousers and socks and boots off the top of the rough capping stones. But in his haste to grab his shirt, he pushed it into the pen.

Renewed alarm filled him.

He threw what clothes he collected to the ground and began to climb the wall once more. But as soon as he got to the top, the Billy goat, having hopped back into the enclosure, now stood up on its hind legs and butted him on the nose immediately his head appeared over the top.

Billy toppled back, straight into a bunch of nettles. 'Ouch! Ouch! Ouch!' he howled as he struggled to get out of them.

When he did get clear he immediately made for the patch of docks growing close by. Soon he was rubbing the juices of the plant into the white blisters already forming on his bare flesh. As he tended to the sores, he looked up. The Billy goat was standing on top of the wall. It was staring down at him with mocking eyes while it chewed contentedly on what remained of his Best Shirt.

Utter despair filled Billy. He drew on his short flannel trousers and clasped his snake belt together and then pulled on his socks and boots. He felt like crying, but his anger and frustration wouldn't allow him to. But what his mum would say when he got into the house he didn't even want to contemplate.

The walk through the village proved to be undignified in the extreme. Though a lot of grown-ups just gazed curiously at him, his greatest misfortune was to bump into Shirley Grimshaw, Monica Pane and Betty Mayley. They were playing hopscotch on the level bit of tarmac outside Mrs Buyer's shop. It required tremendous restraint on his part to bear their giggles and snide remarks as he walked past them, bare-chested, his hair and body still stained vivid yellow by the ochre.

When he got home he found his dad was snoring in his armchair, his mouth wide-open. His granddad, on the other hand, was in his armchair, on the opposite side of the open range. As usual on a Sunday afternoon he was reading *The People* newspaper and was smoking his after-dinner Player's Weights cigarette. He smoked five a day – one after every meal and one at bedtime.

His granddad didn't look at him, but he did cough and rustle his newspaper before he continued reading it. Billy knew it was his granddad's way of showing his displeasure. And that, more than anything else, hurt him terribly. He really didn't like letting his granddad down.

His mother came in from the kitchen. She was wiping her hands free of flour on a piece of cloth. Billy knew she always made scones on a Sunday afternoon for Sunday tea and she usually allowed him to scrape out the basin as a special treat. But as soon as he saw her face he knew his chances of doing that today were zero.

'Where've you been?' she demanded, and then her eyes rounded in dismay when she saw the state he was in. 'What on earth have you been doing? And where is the rest of your good clothes?'

Billy poured out the explanation in a torrent of words. He repeatedly said he was sorry and vowed umpteen times it would never happen again.

'You've been riding on a donkey?' his mum said. She was clearly ignoring his fervent apologies.

'It stopped and chucked me into the Ochre Brook,' he wailed. 'I couldn't stop it. It wasn't my fault.'

'It never is,' his mother said, still obviously fuming.

She got hold of him and cuffed him round the ear and pushed him forcefully towards the kitchen. 'In there this minute and get out of those clothes and get into that bath, you dirty little devil.'

'But there's no hot water!' howled Billy,

'I've no sympathy,' said his mum. 'Get in there.'

'Can't you light the boiler?' Billy implored, staring meaningfully at the cold copper boiler bricked into the far corner of the kitchen. The fire grate was cold and empty underneath it.

'D' you think we're made of money,' his mum demanded, 'lighting fires under the boiler on a Sunday? It's cold water for you my lad, and you'll like it.'

'I won't,' Billy said. 'I've just had one ducking.'

'Serves you right,' his mum said. 'I've no sympathy.'

'But, I haven't had me dinner,' Billy now pointed out.

'And you're not getting any,' his mum said, 'that went into the dustbin an hour ago dried up. Now get out of those clothes.'

Knowing it was no use arguing. Billy unclipped his snake belt and let his trousers fall to the floor

His mum said, 'And come morning I want you out of that bed and fill that boiler with water from the tap and make the fire under it. Are you listening?'

'I'll be late for me newspaper round,' howled Billy.

'You should have thought of that,' his mum said, 'And after you've done that you can get down that cellar and top up the coal bucket.'

Billy wailed, 'But Mr Belham doesn't like me being late.'

'Then you'll have to get up earlier, won't you?'

'Who's going to wake me?' pleaded Billy.

'I'll wake you, don't you fret,' his mum said, 'you dirty young monkey. D' you think clothes grow on trees? You've totally ruined your Best Suit.'

Now thoroughly cowed and knowing it was no use arguing, Billy said, 'Is that it, then?'

His mum glared at him. 'No, it is not. Next Saturday, when you've had your breakfast, you'll black lead that range in the living room and emery paper the hinges. I'll give you ruining your Best Suit you little reprobate.'

Billy's stare now was one of abject misery. 'But I do Mrs Bramble's shopping for her on a Saturday morning. It's the only pocket money I get.'

'You'll have to look sharp then, won't you?' his mum said.

She opened the back door and lifted down the zinc bathtub hanging on a four-inch nail on the outside wall, by the door. She put it in the middle of the kitchen floor and began filling it with water from the brass cold tap over the slop stone, using a galvanized bucket.

When it was fall she said, 'Get in!'

Misery swamped Billy, The shock of the cold water as he gingerly entered it made him instantly shiver after the fierce heat of the day outside.

His mum picked up his ruined clothes.

'I washed them best I could,' he said, hope rising like a

resurrected flame. It was soon extinguished.

'You call this washing?' his mum demanded. 'These are fit for nothing but the dustbin.'

Billy hung his head once more. 'I'm sorry mum, I won't do it again. I promise. Honest.'

His mum sighed. 'Where have I heard that before?' But there was softness to her tone now and he knew the storm was over.

But he still felt wretched as he got to work with the green bar of carbolic soap. It stung his abrasions and set his white nettle pimples throbbing again. But he bore the pain with fortitude for the sake of his mum.

The following week things picked up. Monday evening his old friend, Owd Isaac, who lived in a shed in Grin Wood, gave him a sixpenny piece for cleaning out his four hen cotes while he went out setting some rabbit hangs. Tuesday evening, Mrs Bramble paid him a shilling for shovelling a ton of coal into her cellar. With the money he bought a box of chocolates and gave them to his mum. His mum gave him a big hug and a big kiss, which he tried unsuccessfully to avoid.

But, regarding Jerusalem's Cuckoo...

It was the following Friday afternoon. He was in the playground with Wesley Ward and the gang. It was during the mid-afternoon break. They were all leaning against the toilet wall making derisive remarks as they watched the girls play at skipping. But when their jeering palled he said to Wesley, 'I haven't heard Jerusalem's Cuckoo making any noise today.'

'That's because he's gone,' Wesley said gloomily.

Billy stared, 'Eh?'

Wesley looked at him, his eyes sad. 'Me dad said it's economics.'

Billy frowned. 'What's economics?'

Wesley shrugged. 'Summat to do with money,' he said. 'Me dad said some of his best customers for eggs and goat's milk live around Ann Croft and he couldn't afford to lose them. He said he could make much more money out of selling such things than I could carting things using Jerusalem's Cuckoo. For a start, he said it was costing him a fortune for graze. So last night, he sold the cart and Jerusalem's Cuckoo to Owd Walter Prewett up Ladmanlow.'

Billy said, 'What did your mum say to that?'

'She said she were glad to see the back of it after all the trouble it had caused,' Wesley said.

'So that's it then,' Billy said.

Wesley nodded. 'Looks like it.'

Billy said, 'What happens now?'

Wesley shrugged again and then produced a packet of Woodbine cigarettes from his trouser pocket.

'We could have a smoke in t' toilets,' he said.

Billy shook his head. 'Oh, not me, mate,' he said. 'It stinks to high heaven in there this time of year.'

'In Grin Wood tonight, then,' said Wesley.

'Aye, that's more like it,' Billy said. 'I've no stick chopping on.'

The rest of the gang agreed wholeheartedly. In fact they became so enthusiastic they went back to jeering at the girls again until the bell went, calling them in.

CHAPTER SIX

THE TALES OF OWD OLIVER

It was a boiling hot Saturday afternoon in the middle of July, Billy was walking down St John's Road to Buxton. The gang was trailing behind him, clearly feeling the heat. They were on their way to watch the Wells Dressing Parade – a colourful pageant that more or less ended the Blessing of the Wells Festivities, which started on Wednesday and finished on Saturday.

Billy knew Buxton was called the Spa of Blue Waters and that the Romans lived here at one time and built baths to wash and heal themselves in. However, then, they called the town Aquae Arnemetiae and Billy also understood that Mary, Queen of Scots, stayed at the Old Hall Hotel to take the waters to cure her rheumatism – before they chopped her head off, that is. But that, he decided, was beside the point at the moment for there were much more important matters to deal with.

He turned to the gang strung out behind him along the pavement.

'Come on,' he shouted, 'or we'll miss the Procession.'

When he slouched up to him, hands in pockets, Hump Bramble said, 'I'm not running, it's too blinking hot.'

Winker Benton arrived and said, 'Well I d-don't mind r-running a bit. We w-want to get a g - good place b - before t' Parade starts, d - don't we?'

Wesley Ward, who had been matching Billy pace for pace, said, 'How about running a lamp and walking a lamp?'

'Yeh,' Billy said, and then frowned around at the other gang members. 'Glad somebody can come up with an idea.'

Hump Bramble said, scowling across at him, 'Aye, well, it makes a change from having thee coming up with them, doesn't it?'

The Green brothers, who were leaning against the hawthorn hedge nearby dripping sweat, seemed to be just waiting for somebody to make a decision. It was as if by silent agreement, despite the reservations of some, the gang began running to the next gas lamppost down the road, then walk to the next and so on until they finally got to Buxton. Even so, Hump Bramble still managed to moan most of the way. Indeed, even when they found a good position outside the Royal Vaults on Spring Gardens and wormed their way to the front of the jostling crowd, Hump wasn't satisfied, even though nobody was taking notice of him any more.

Now standing on the kerbside with the crowds Billy realised the atmosphere around him was seething with anticipation. Everywhere was the constant hubbub of excited voices. And elated expectancy shone on every exuberant face he could see. Topping that, gaily-dressed vendors were walking up and down the crowd, keeping up a steady banter while urging people to buy their wares. For hard cash the sellers would dispense balloons and flags, tooters and bunting. Then they would place the purchased goods into the hands of small, delighted children who immediately began to wave them, or toot them, or shake them.

Watching them Billy found slight resentment filling him. He didn't have any money to buy anything, but, dwelling on it, he didn't think he would have wasted his cash on that stuff anyway – not with the Funfair going full swing up on the Market Place at this very moment. His money would have gone on the Dodgems or the Waltzer, or the Roll Penny stalls, or whatever new speciality ride was being introduced this year.

But crashing into his thoughts, and sending his pulses racing anew, Billy now heard the distant BOOM! BOOM! ... BOOM, BOOM, BOOM! of a big bass drum striking up. The noise was coming from the direction of Fairfield, carried on the hot breeze wafting across the town and fluttering the flags suspended like a forest above the whole length of Spring Gardens.

The noise of the big drum suggested to Billy that the awards of

First, Second, Third and Highly Commended for the Tableaux or Best Entrants were decided and the formalities of presentation by the Mayor were over. Now, the Wells Dressing Parade – and the band chosen to lead it – was ready to begin their march through town.

Billy found he could hardly restrain himself from stamping his feet and swinging his arms to the beat of the military march as it struck up, even though it was still faint in the distance. And with the rousing noises of the band blaring into life, the buzz from the crowd lifted to a throb of growing expectation.

Captured by the excitement Billy leaned forward eagerly, his eyes shining and waited with baited breath for his first sight of the oncoming Parade.

The main shopping concourse, he observed during the wait, was now even more packed with excited people, no doubt swelled by the pubs emptying in order to allow the former imbibers to watch the show. They were mostly men with pint pots held in their worked-gnarled hands. Most of them were limestone quarrymen, he knew. It was the main industry in these parts.

But above the shops and pubs along the street, Billy observed more people were leaning out of the rising ranks of upstairs windows, in preparation to wave their flags and cheer. Some, he saw, were already pointing in the direction of the Viaduct at the bottom of the Spring Gardens. He assumed they were, like him, eagerly awaiting the first sight of the Grand Parade.

Within a few minutes he saw the first of the Procession come swinging into view round the bend at the bottom of Fairfield Road. The band and the beginnings of the Procession were soon marching under the Viaduct past Elliot's Toyshop, the Toilets at the Bottom of Bridge Street and the Children's Well, then on past the Co-op, Sanders Garage and the Spa Cinema.

Now he could distinguish the drum majorettes behind the lead band. They reminded him of toy soldiers in their pristine uniforms of red and cream and cockaded tall hats with their shiny peaks. They were all girls, he observed, and they were moving their arms in synchronised movements and slapping their thighs and saluting. Billy also observed, as they came ever nearer, their thighs appeared to be already red-raw from the punishment they were receiving from the slapping. But the girls didn't seem to mind, or they hid it very well if they did.

In what seemed no time at all, the lead band was rasping past him, making ready to wheel right at the head of Spring Gardens to progress towards the Quadrant. The bandsmen, he observed, were already red faced and sweating copiously. And their cheeks ballooned in and out as they blew on their instruments, which flashed brassily in the glorious sunlight streaming down.

Following the band and the drum majorettes came a troupe of girls and boys bashing their tambourines and rattling their kettledrums and razzing their bazookas and looking very smart in their outfits. Behind them came the St John's Ambulance Brigade, then more dancers. Then the Red Cross nurses, the Cubs, the Scouts, the Brownies and the Girl Guides. And dispersed between them were more troupes of dancers, another brass band. And spaced between them were the beautifully presented tableaux, the dressed-up people on them displaying the different themes they represented, some extremely funny, some more serious. And constantly cavorting in between those slow-moving platforms were more gaily-dressed people.

Individuals were dancing, smiling, waving and appealing to the crowds on both sides of the street to give generously to the charities or causes they were collecting for. They dressed as clowns, or Mickey and Minnie Mouse, or Charlie Chaplin, or Laurel and Hardy, or Robin Hood, or The Three Bears, et al. They danced and pranced and acted the fool, taking liberties they wouldn't normally dream of taking as they weaved their way between the tableaux and rattled their charity tins under peoples' noses exhorting them to give generously. But winning the day for Billy was the Roman soldier, who was clad in gleaming armour and mounted on a prancing white horse. He was tremendous, Now came the Buxton Festival Queen's tableau. Billy decided she was the loveliest girl he had ever seen, in the prettiest dress he had ever seen. And she was smiling radiantly and waving to everybody. He grinned and waved back, but she didn't seem to notice him. However, that disappointment was soon forgotten when more brass bands came swinging into view, waving their trombones and blowing their cornets and trumpets. He noted the bands' names while admiring their panache as they marched past or marked time to allow the rear of the Procession to catch up.

There were bands from Harpur Hill, Dove Holes, Peak Dale, Chapel-en-le-frith, Whaley Bridge and New Mills. There was a band from Hollins Clough and one from Longnor. There was even a band from Flash, or Quarnford to give it its proper name. Sandwiched between them were more high-stepping, thigh-slapping majorettes and more tambourine-bashing bands. Spread out between them were the Rose Queens' floats – beautiful girls from other towns and villages throughout the High Peak.

Then Burbage Silver Prize Band came marching by. Billy soon picked out his granddad. He was marching along, his glass eye watering and his military-style hat set at a rakish angle. His music was clipped to his trombone and his sergeant-major moustache – made ginger with nicotine stain – was flaring and receding each time he blew. Immense pride filled Billy and he frantically waved to attract his granddad's attention, but he didn't seem to notice him. Nevertheless, Billy continued to wave and shout until the last float, troupe and band passed by and the razzmatazz noises of the Grand Parade faded into the distance toward the Devonshire Royal Hospital and St John's Road, on to make a full circuit of the town.

The intense electric atmosphere that had built up, Billy now realised, was dispersing and the throng around him was breaking up. But everybody was still abuzz with excited talk. Most of the people, Billy noticed, were heading for the Market Place, no doubt to go on the Fair.

Along with the gang Billy followed the crowd to the head of Spring Gardens, where the main shopping street joined with Terrace Road, There, near the Toilets below the Taxi Rank – under the shade of the big chestnut tree at the bottom of the Slopes – Billy paused and looked into the faces of the gang, 'Well, what d'you think?' he said, to nobody in particular.

Wesley Ward sniffed, stuck his hands in his trouser pockets and shrugged. 'It were all right, I suppose. But some of the floats weren't up to much, were they?'

Winker Benton, bright-eyed, said, 'W - well, I thought it w - were grand; the b - best Procession 've ever s - seen.'

Percy Green said, 'I reckon the one last year was better.'

Hump Bramble grumbled, 'I thought we were going up to t' Fair, after the Procession were over?' Hump was leaning against the Toilet wall picking his nose and inspecting the crow it produced before flicking it away.

Billy, now realising he must disclose the embarrassing position he didn't mention before said, 'I can't. I've got no money.'

Indeed, it came as a big shock to him earlier in the day when Mrs Bramble said she didn't want her shopping done this week. He was depending on the money she would give him so he could go to the Fair. She was going shopping with her sister, she said, who was up from Ashford-in-the-Water especially to see the Wells and the Procession. But being the nice lady she was, Mrs Bramble did thank him very much for calling and hoped he would be able to do her shopping next week. But the trouble with that was, Billy now thought glumly, you can't spend thanks.

It was then he realised Wesley Ward was patting him on the back. 'Never mind, mate,' he said, 'you can still come with us.' He spread his impish grin. 'Tell you what: I'll help you look under t' penny roll stalls, how's that? There's usually a copper or two under them.' He added, 'I'd lend you some money myself, but I've only got sixpence.'

'A - and I've o - only g - got t - three pence,' said Winker Benton, with equal regret.

'And I've nowt to spare,' Hump Bramble said, 'so don't look at me.'

Eddie Green sniffed and shuffled and looked at the ground. 'And it's no use looking at me, either. I'm near skint.'

'Same here,' said Percy, his brother. 'Four pence, that's all I've got.'

Billy shrugged resignedly, but, really, he felt terrible, utterly miserable to be in such a destitute state. But he said bravely, 'It's all right, I can go and watch them playing tennis in t' Pavilion Gardens. You can come in to me there when you've spent up. Happen we can go climbing trees in Grin Wood after, eh? It'll be cool in there.'

'That's not much – watching tennis,' Wesley said.

'I like watching it,' Billy said.

'Oh, aye?' said Wesley. It was clear he knew he was lying.

'He's going to watch them women in their short skirts, that's what he's going to do,' said Hump Bramble. He grinned. 'Aren't tha, Billy?'

Eddie Green laughed, 'Yeh! The dirty bugger.'

'No, I'm not!' said Billy and blushed. He blushed quite often, at the slightest thing. 'I'm not like you beggars,' he continued, glaring, 'gawping at ladies bloomers on washing lines and watching for what sort of knickers the girls are wearing.'

'Take no notice of them,' Wesley said 'Tell you what, mate; I'll stay with you. I'm not all that bothered about going on t' Fair anyway.'

Warm feelings instantly welled up in Billy. 'Aw, thanks, pal,' he said. 'But it wouldn't be right, spoiling your fun.'

Wesley shrugged, 'Well, t' offer's there if you want it.'

'Well, we can't stand here all day talking,' said Hump Bramble. Then he urged, with unusual concern, 'Come on. Billy, watching t' Fair going round'll be better than watching ruddy tennis.'

'Aye,' said Eddie Green, 'owt 's better than that.'

'I'm all right,' Billy lied again.

Percy Green shrugged. 'Well, don't say we didn't ask.'

Billy watched as the gang went running and whooping and weaving their way through the droves of people walking up the stiff slope of Terrace Road to the Market Place. But all the time he observed them he felt a deepening despondency sinking like a lump of lead into the pit of his stomach. However, he eventually managed to pull himself together. He trudged along with the crowds walking along the bottom of The Slopes. But he did pause to look at the Dressed Well next to the Pump Room. He gazed at it with some pride. He knew his mum helped to make this one. She once explained to him how they created the pictures that were so admired by visitors and locals alike. The method used, she said, was to press flower petals and leaves and such like into a damp clay back. Exacting work that needed a lot of patience, she explained, but the results in the end were very rewarding. This particular picture depicted MOSES STRIKING THE ROCK. Billy put his hands behind his back while be admired it. It was a really grand depiction of that biblical event and he did have a comparison in his mind he could call upon. He'd seen a similar picture in his granddad's large, Illustrated Family Bible. But the real delight for him lay in the fact that his mum helped to make it.

Now on Broad Walk Billy headed for the ginnel that connected the Walk with Burlington Road, thus splitting the Pavilion Gardens in two. The whole of the Gardens was enclosed using spiked five-foot iron railings. At the second bridge that passed over the ginnel, he stopped and looked furtively up and down to see if anybody was coming. Nobody was. He took a deep breath, then, with practiced ease, got purchase with his pumps on the grim railings and climbed over. He dropped safely amongst the shiny-leaved rhododendrons and laurels on the other side. Quickly picking himself up he pushed through the tangled bushes and scrambled on to the nearest path. Some people, walking past, looked at him curiously as he emerged from the shrubbery. He blushed with guilt before he scurried away.

Within a couple of minutes he was sitting on a seat near the Tennis Courts. But really, if he was going to be entirely honest with himself, he was here not because he wanted to watch the tennis, but because he wanted to sulk. However, he soon found his torment wasn't over

He stared at Owd Oliver Butterworth. He was approaching him from the direction of the Conservatory. He was clearly making a bee-line for him, using his walking stick to propel him along as fast possible. His dad said he should listen to Owd Oliver diligently (whatever that meant) because he might learn summat.

'Now then, lad,' Owd Oliver said, grinning down at him and exposing the gaps in his yellow and worn-down teeth.

'Now then,' Billy said unenthusiastically.

Owd Oliver was dressed in his customary garb. Flat brown cap shoved back on to the top of his high-domed head, a tuft of silver-grey hair frothing out from under the peak. And Owd Oliver's nose, Billy now observed, looked larger and redder and knobbier than ever he'd seen it and the purple veins that streaked it appeared to be even more pronounced than usual. Even the hairs that grew out of each flared nostril looked longer and greyer And it was well known Owd Oliver wasn't the best of dressers. About the old man's scrawny neck was the perennial off-white silk scarf. It was tucked into his not-too-clean white-and-blue striped collarless shirt, which was wide open at his whiskery neck. It had a brass collar stud attached to one eyelet, though Billy had never seen him actually wear a collar – paper or celluloid. But, the most striking thing about Owd Oliver, Billy always thought, was his height, six foot five if he were an inch. His granddad once told him that, when Owd Oliver was not much more than a boy, he joined the Guards as a regular soldier and fought in the Boer War – whatever that was – as well as the Great War, which Billy did know a little about.

Another striking thing about Owd Oliver, Billy decided now, though he'd often seen it before, was the old man's thick black overcoat. Summer or winter – hail, rain or shine – it seemed Owd Oliver chose to wear that long, stained garment. Indeed, the coat was so lengthy it nearly touched the ground. But not because it was naturally long but because some thick grey-and-black striped material had, at one time, been sewn on to the bottom of it. Owd Oliver once told him that the extra length was there to keep his legs warm during winter, because his trousers were thin. But, Billy now ruminated, that didn't explain why Owd Oliver wore it during the summer. Perhaps it was the only coat he owned? Perhaps he had nowt on underneath? But there was another odd thing about Owd Oliver, studied Billy, it was his eyes. The tawny brown pupils had white rings round them. And the part that should have been white was a jaundiced yellow.

'Move up, lad,' Owd Oliver was saying, waving his brass-ferruled stick, 'make a bit of room for an owd 'un.'

Though there was plenty of room on the bench Billy moved along. In a way he was glad to have some distance between himself and the old man, because sometimes Owd Oliver could smell a bit ripe.

Owd Oliver sat – or, more like, descended – upon the seat with a deep sigh. 'Aaaah,' he sighed, 'that's better, lad. T'owd legs aren't what they used to be, tha knows?' Now he grinned and leaned over. 'It's Peter Nobstick's grandson, isn't it?'

Owd Oliver's breath, Billy found, smelled very strongly of beer.

'Yes,' he said.

'Been watching t' Procession?' Owd Oliver raised his white eyebrows, as if in enquiry.

Billy thought the brows looked like two fat, hairy caterpillars; 'Yes,' he said.

'Not going up t' Fair, then?' Owd Oliver said.

'No.'

'I see,' Owd Oliver frowned and then added, with a grin, 'You've not a lot to say for yourself, has t' lad?'

'I'm watching t' tennis,' Billy said.

'Oh, aye.' Owd Oliver looked towards the courts. 'Nowt else better to do they haven't. More money than sense, some of them.'

'Have they?' Billy said, and began wondering how anybody could have more money than sense. He thought it took a lot of sense to earn some money.

But Owd Oliver said, 'Mark my words.'

He began breathing rapidly, and then he began to cough. It was a bubbling cough that seemed to begin somewhere deep within his chest. Eventually he ceased his wheezing and hawked up phlegm and turned and looked around for somewhere to deposit it. When he appeared to find the right spot he sent a stream of the yellow matter splashing into the rhododendron bushes behind them.

'Aaaah! Her's better out than in,' he said, and then explained, tapping his chest, 'It's t' tobacco, lad. You'd do well to leave that stuff alone is my advice. It stunts your growth for one thing, does tobacco.'

'Oh,' Billy said, and immediately wondered why Owd Oliver had grown so tall if that was the case.

'What did you think of t' Procession?' Owd Oliver was saying.

'It were all right, I suppose,' Billy said.

'Only 'all right'?' Owd Oliver hoisted his shaggy eyebrows in astonishment.

'Yes,' Billy said.

Owd Oliver rubbed his nose. 'Aye, well, I've got to admit the Festivals aren't what they used to be, lad. Oh, no. At one time, tha knows, all the streets were decked up solid with garlands – made from thousands of flowers, all hand-fashioned out of rolls of coloured crepe paper.'

'I know,' Billy said.

'Happen tha does, lad, happen tha does. Did thee granddad tell thee?'

'Yes.'

'But then' – Owd Oliver paused to describe a huge arc with his right arm – 'they used to make these great arches out of wooden trellis and wire netting. Then they would erect them at each end of the street. They made a wondrous gateway to the street, lad – truly a sight to behold. Some would have GOD SAVE THE KING woven into them with white crepe flowers, or some other appropriate colour while the rest of the frame was covered with other like things. And if t' lass they picked to be the Festival Queen lived on that particular street' – Billy jumped as Owd Oliver grinned heartily and brought his brass-ferruled walking stick down to the tarmac with a resounding thump – 'why, lad, there would be a show to behold! Crepe flowers – reds, yellows, greens, blues, whites, pinks, you name it – all woven into the trelliswork and secured with bits of wire and describing GOOD LUCK TO MARY or ELSIE or whatever else t' lass's name happened to be – and GOD BLESS HER.'

Owd Oliver's rheumy eyes became alive and shone with enthusiasm as he warmed to his tale. 'Why, every house used to be decked up, lad,' he said; 'cloth flags slung across t' streets – bedroom window to bedroom window. And the floats they used to have – why, they were a real sight to see. Artistry personified.'

Owd Oliver paused and leaned over confidentially. 'Buxton Corporation always did the Queens tableau, lad,' he said, 'and they used their best horses to pull it. Big, fine cart horses they were – the ones they usually use to pull t' snowploughs and refuse carts with, but groomed and curried for the occasion until they shone like buttons.'

Billy felt Owd Walters hand rest gently on his shoulder. 'They had to use those horses, lad, because they had the strength in them, dost see? They needed to pull some weight did them horses, I can tell thee. Think of it, lad: the float were a ton or more for a start – then, with all the Maids in Waiting on it, as well as t' Queen… well, it weren't a job for the weak.'

'Suppose not,' Billy said.

Owd Oliver nodded his head vigorously and then his gaze reached far away, as if he was remembering a time long gone. 'Aye, what grand horses they were, lad,' he said. 'Hung with brasses that gleamed like gold in the sun, and harness that was polished so brightly you could see your face in it. And the Fairs on t' Market, lad,' he went on, 'even if you didn't have any money for a ride, it didn't matter because you could always go and watch them steam engines working. Big, thumping things they were, with long leather belts to drive the generators, as well as numerous other things. Steam hissed out of brass valves and grease and oil and water dripped out all over t' place, making big pools under the machines, forcing them to put sawdust down to soak it all up. Oh, aye, and they smelt glorious did them engines, lad. Top o' that, what a sight they were at night! The boiler fires casting light into the sky when they opened the doors up to fuel them with coal – the light bouncing off the clouds if they were low enough.'

Owd Walter leaned back and smiled fondly. 'Aye, they used to belch out great columns of smoke did them steam engines, lad, and clank and hiss and gasp as though they were alive. Then there were t' steam organs. You could hear them jazzing out their tunes as far away as Fairfield, or Burbage, or Harpur Hill. It were just one big, grand show was t' fair, lad, in them days!'

'Was it?' Billy said.

He wasn't bored exactly, but the Fair Owd Oliver was describing wasn't much different to the one now. The only difference was they mostly used diesel engines to power the generators, instead of steam engines with their big leather belts.

Owd Oliver went silent and lighted his pipe. While he did Billy watched the two men that were playing tennis come off one of the courts and enter the pavilion. Moments later two more players came bouncing out of the building. They sprinted down the steps and out on to the vacant playing area.

Three young ladies in white skirts and striped blouses, sitting on the veranda with fruit drinks in their hands, were giggling and chattering and pointing at the men's backs as they went on to the court. One of the men turned and called something, which sent the girls into a hand-cupped, tittering huddle.

His pipe well lighted, and clouds of smoke blooming up everywhere, Owd Oliver turned and spat a stream of spittle into the rhododendron bushes. His pipe crackled vigorously as he drew on it. It clearly wanted cleaning. But, having got it well lighted the old man leaned back with a sigh and supported his right arm by cupping the elbow in his left hand. He held his pipe by the stem, between his thumb and first finger.

'Dost go to the pictures, lad?' he said presently, staring down.

'Oh, yes,' Billy said.

'Hmm, well, they don't make films like they used to, tha knows?' informed Owd Walter firmly, blowing a cloud of blue-white smoke into the still air. 'I can remember when they used to have Charlie Chaplin, William S Hart, Douglas Fairbanks and Mary Pickford on at the Hippodrome. In the silent days of course.'

'The silent days?' Billy said. 'What are them?'

'When they didn't talk on t' film, lad,' Owd Oliver said. 'Talking films didn't start until 1928. Al Jolson in the Jazz Singer.'

'Oh,' Billy said. 'Who was Al Jolson? I've seen Charlie Chaplin and Laurel and Hardy,' Billy went on, the mention of films beginning to stir him from his lethargy.

'Oh, aye, you can always have a good laugh at them,' said Owd Oliver with a chuckle, 'but who is your real favourite?'

'Johnny Weismuller.'

'That Tarzan feller?'

'Yes. He can kill lions.'

'Did you know he was an Olympic champion swimmer?' Owd Oliver said.

'What's that?' Billy said.

'It means he was the best in t' world, lad.'

'Yeh, well, he was bound to be,' Billy said, with some pride. Indeed, he often tried to emulate Tarzan by swimming a length of the Public Baths in the Crescent faster than anybody else and swing on ropes suspended from tree branches in Grin Wood. He even yodelled like Tarzan. Not only that he suffered a Green Stick Fracture to his left wrist after his hands slipped off the rope when he was over a fifteen-foot drop. He used a knitting needle to scratch his arm when it was in plaster.

'D' you watch many films, lad?' Owd Oliver said.

'Oh, yes,' Billy said.

'Well, I've got to say I'm a bit partial to Jeanette Macdonald and Nelson Eddy myself.' Owd Oliver went on. 'New Moon and Rose Marie; that sort of stuff, as well as Ginger Rogers and Fred Astaire dancing, of course.'

'Me mum and dad like Ginger Rogers and Fred Astaire,' said Billy. 'They go dancing at the Pavilion Gardens Ballroom.' He pointed at the Octagon close by. 'Me dad says it's a sprung floor and perfect for dancing. He says it's as good as the Tower Ballroom floor at Blackpool. They used to go dancing in competitions there before they got married.'

Owd Walter rubbed his chin and said, 'Well, they've got a few sprung floors in London, lad, now you come to mention it.'

Billy stared. 'Have you been to London?' The farthest he had ever been was Rhyl on a Sunday School Day Trip.

Owd Walter nodded. 'Oh, aye, lad; not only that I've seen the king – the owd one, that is, George the Fifth.'

'Gerrout,' Billy said, sitting up from his slumped position.

'Not only that,' said Owd Oliver, 'when I was in Africa on a tour of duty with the Guards I saw lions and all manner of things.'

'Did you see Tarzan?'

Owd Oliver offered him a smile. 'I did better than that, lad,' he said. 'I saw them lions running down wildebeest and killing them for food. But what sickened me was when t' officers used to shoot lions and water buffalos and other beast with their high-powered rifles, just so they could put their foot on them to make out how brave they were.' The old man paused and shook his head sadly. 'Though I'm not squeamish, I never thought there was anything very brave about such conduct. No.' Owd Oliver paused again and spat into the bushes. 'Now, the Masai tribesmen, on the other hand,' he continued, 'they used to kill lions with just their spears. But there was a reason. It was because the lions killed their cows and goats. There was great respect between the two species. In fact the boys of the tribe were obliged to kill a lion single-handed before they could be looked upon as men. Just think of that, lad. No more than fourteen years old maybe and with only a spear or two to defend themselves with. Now, *that's* what I call bravery.' The old man's pipe crackled as he pulled on it and then he stared pensively at the people playing tennis, as though he was again remembering days long past, 'Good days them were, lad – well, most of them, anyway.'

'What about elephants?' Billy said. 'Did you see any elephants?'

Owd Oliver looked down at him delight in his rheumy eyes. 'Magnificent animals they are, lad,' he said, 'beautiful and intelligent.' Then the old man shook his head and his gaze took on a hard edge. 'But the beggars had to shoot them, too. I often wondered what they would do if they put a spear in *their* hands and asked them to kill, man to beast, as it were. I think it'd be a different tale then.' Owd Oliver shook his head sadly. 'What a terrible waste of life it were.'

'Didn't Tarzan stop them?' Billy said,

Owd Oliver smiled indulgently, 'No, lad, not as I know of. I reckon he must have been somewhere else at the time.'

It was then Billy saw the gang trooping towards him – past the section of the Wye River that was dammed to form the Paddling Pool.

'Here's me mates,' he said.

Owd Oliver raised his brows. 'Oh, right,' he said. 'You'll be off then.'

Billy nodded. 'But I'd like to talk to you again sometime… about Africa.'

'Tickled your fancy did that, eh, lad?' Owd Oliver said,

'Yes.'

Owd Walter grinned. 'Right, we'll have to see about it then, won't we?'

'Yes.'

Owd Oliver now began fishing about in his extra-long overcoat pocket. 'You've got no money, have you, lad?' he said.

Billy stared. 'How d'you know?'

Owd Oliver grinned. 'Oh, I know, lad,' he said. 'I weren't born yesterday.' He pulled his hand out of his overcoat pocket and flipped something into the air. Billy caught it as it came spinning down. It was a bright shilling. 'Now then,' Owd Walter said, 'dost think you can make a hole in that, up at that Fair?'

Billy looked down at a twelve pence piece, then back up at Owd Oliver. 'But, I've done nowt to earn it,' he said.

'Shall I take it back, then?' Owd Oliver said.

'I didn't mean that, I meant –'

Owd Oliver grinned and patted his arm. 'I know what tha meant, lad. Now, get off with thee.'

Billy found he was reluctant to say goodbye, but he did and got up and waved at the gang to follow him as he raced across the lawns, past the Band Stand in which Peak Dale Band was playing, then across the bridge and on towards the turnstile at the bottom of Fountain Street.

As be ran past the Police Station at the top of the street the noise from the Fair became a thunderous din: the jangle of popular tunes; the thumping of steam and diesel engines; the babble of a thousand voices melding into a throbbing cacophony of life and colour. Three cheers for Owd Oliver, Billy thought gleefully as he dashed towards the Dodgems.

Three weeks later he heard Owd Oliver died – of neglect, Billy's granddad said.

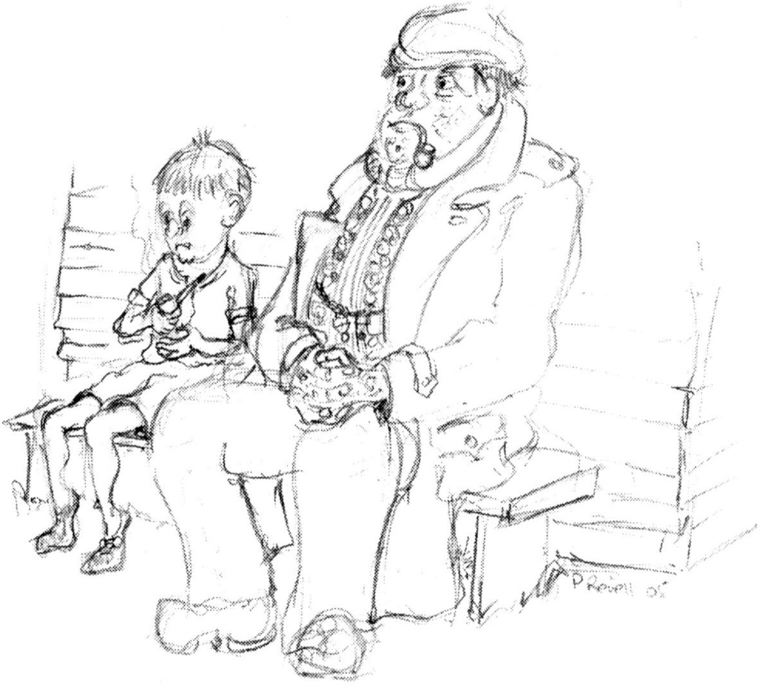

CHAPTER SEVEN

THROWING UP IN FRONT OF OWD ISAAC

Sitting here in Grin Wood with Owd Isaac, Billy was feeling relaxed, almost to the point of being lethargic. The school Summer Holidays were almost over, the Wells Dressings celebrations a memory, and this particular boiling hot August day was now settling down to become a pleasant, if not balmy, evening.

He was thinking about this afternoon. He spent it with the gang fishing for sticklebacks in the stream that came from under the ground at Wye Head and meandered through Wye Fields, before it went into the Pavilion Gardens Boating Lake. He was so successful he caught a jam jar full of minnows and sticklebacks. They were now at home – still in the jar – standing on the dressing table in the attic bedroom.

He gazed up at the deep green canopy. The evening sunlight was dappling down through gaps. Owd Isaac, as usual, was sitting beside him on the long wooden bench that was drawn up against one of the four tarred, felt-covered hen cotes Owd Isaac owned. The old man was resting his back against the west side of the building. His eyes were closed. He appeared to be dozing.

Billy scratched his nose. He couldn't make his mind up whether he was unhappy or not, sitting here with Owd Isaac. The gang, he knew, were down Buxton at the Opera House, watching what they said was a good film. He couldn't join them because, as usual, he'd got no money.

He gazed at the contours of his old friend's face. To him Owd Isaac appeared to be a block of ancient, gnarled oak – crouched and solid, even though he was only fifty five years old. And his face could be likened to a brown prune into which were set two merry eyes of vivid blue.

His mother often said Owd Isaac looked as if he needed a good wash. Billy screwed up his pliable face to think about that. Well, he had to admit Owd Isaac's craggy chin did have a covering of grey, tobacco-stained stubble on it. And his tanned face did look as though it needed a good lathering from time to time.

Billy toyed with the willow switch in his hand, with which he occasionally scooped up individual dead leaves with and flirted them into the air to see how far they would float – usually not very far for the air was too still. However, on reflection, Billy reckoned the real feature of Owd Isaac's makeup was his battered briar pipe. It always seemed to be sticking out of his wide, purple-lipped mouth. Indeed, it was such a permanent fixture Billy often wondered if Owd Isaac went to bed with it still stuck in his mouth…

Owd Isaac suddenly roused himself. 'You haven't a lot to say for yourself, lad. Has t' cat got thee tongue?'

Billy always thought Owd Isaac's voice sounded like rough sandpaper being rasped across wood that had not been planed.

'Me mates have gone to t' pictures,' he said,

Owd Isaac sniffed. 'Oh, I see. It's like that, is it?' The old man looked sidewise at him, the light of amusement in his eyes, which Billy resented a little. 'Hmm, well,' Owd Isaac went on, 'we'll have to see if we can do summat about that, won't we?'

'Like what?' Billy said.

'I'm thinking about it,' Owd Isaac said.

He eased up from the hen cote he was leaning his back against and added, 'As a matter of fact, I'm glad you called in to see me, lad. I've been wanting to pass summat on to thee for some time.'

Curious, Billy also came up from his slumped position on the wooden bench and stared at his old companion,

'Like what?' he said.

Owd Isaac began rummaging about in one of the capacious pockets in his long brown coat. He eventually produced a brand new clay pipe. Billy saw the end of the stem was still painted a bright red.

Owd Isaac beamed down at him, 'Now then,' he said, 'what d'you think of that? I said I'd get thee one and here it is.'

Billy stared at the magnificent pipe with some amazement. 'I thought you were joking,' he said,

'Well, you were wrong, weren't you?' Owd Isaac said.

A bubbling, phlegm-filled laugh gurgled somewhere deep down in his chest. He leaned over and offered him the pipe. 'Here, get hold of it,' he said.

Billy took the pipe and gazed at it. 'You really mean I can keep it?' he said.

'What dost think I mean?' Owd Isaac said, arching his brows. 'And if you're worried about your folks seeing it, you can always keep it here.'

'I'm not old enough to smoke,' Billy said.

'Oh, aye?' said Owd Isaac. 'Since when has that stopped thee?'

'I've never smoked a pipe,' Billy said.

'Well, there's nowt to it,' said Owd Isaac. 'You just suck on it the same as you would a fag. You smoke cigarettes, don't you?'

'Sometimes.'

Once more the old man began rummaging about in his pockets.

Billy watched and wondered what was going to appear next. Rumour in the village had it that Owd Isaac was 'worth a bit'; that he didn't have to wander about like a tramp doing odd jobs and living in his ten by eight shed next to his hen cotes, which had a small pot-bellied stove installed in one corner to keep him warm in winter. Indeed, gleaned from some crafty eavesdropping and casual questioning, Billy also learned that, once upon a time, before the World War, Owd Isaac owned a scrap metal business and made a lot of money from it. But when he came back from the Conflict he was suffering from what was called 'shell shock', which, some said, left him a bit strange. Even so, despite his poor health, it was said he did try to pick up the pieces of his life again and carry on with his business. But then it was said Owd Isaac received another blow. His wife left him and went to live with a Rascal in Manchester,

The suddenness of her departure, apparently, nearly killed Owd Isaac. And it was soon after that shattering event that he decided to sell his business to go and live in Grin Wood. However, he did eventually get over his troubles. Indeed, he often said his one big regret in life was that he didn't have any children but he never married again.

'Now then,' Owd Isaac said, 'let's see if we can get that pipe going.'

From his pocket he produced an OXO tin from which most of the paintwork had been worn off with long use, to expose the shiny metal underneath.

'There's twist in here, lad,' Owd Isaac said, waving the tin under his nose; 'it's the purest tobacco tha can get. Never do thee harm. Ask any quarryman. They chew it as well as smoke it. Why,' Owd Isaac went on, 'Owd Percy Prewett up Ladmanlow has smoked it all his life and look at him – he's ninety if he's a day.' Owd Isaac tapped his forehead knowingly. 'Keeps thee brain as fresh as a daisy does twist, lad, and don't let anybody tell thee otherwise.'

Billy frowned. 'How does it do that?'

Owd Isaac screwed up his rubbery face. 'I don't really know. It just does, that's all.' He shook his head. 'Tha does ask some daft questions sometimes. Is thee brain never still?'

'Mum says I'm too curious,' Billy said.

'Curious, eh?' Owd Isaac chuckled. 'Well, you know what curiosity did, don't you, lad?'

'No.'

'It killed the cat.'

'How can it do that?'

'Cats are curious, lad,' said Owd Isaac, 'and because they are it usually gets them into trouble. That's why they've got nine lives.'

Billy frowned, 'How can anything have nines lives?'

Owd Isaac sighed, then chuckled. 'I'm beginning to see what tha mum means,' he said. 'Now shut thee cake hole a minute and pay attention.'

He snapped open the lid of the OXO tin in his hand and pulled out a thin rope of black, tarry-looking tobacco. He beamed. 'This is t' stuff, lad; pig tail!'

Billy frowned again. 'It doesn't look like a pig's tail.'

Owd Isaac said, 'It's just a name they've give it, damn it.'

'Ok.'

Owd Isaac raised his grey brows. 'Hast done now?'

'Yes,' Billy said. 'I were just wondering, that's all.'

'That's thee trouble,' said Owd Isaac and then he grinned. 'But tha wouldn't be bright if you didn't ask questions, would you, lad?'

'That's what me granddad says.'

Owd Isaac plunged the hand not holding the pipe into the depths of his greatcoat pocket. While he fumbled about, Billy's gaze went to the familiar swell of Owd Isaac's stomach. His food-stained red-and-cream patterned waistcoat covered it. Under the waistcoat was his blue and white striped collarless cotton shirt, open at the neck. Across Owd Isaac's gaudy waistcoat rested the heavy silver watch chain. From the middle dangled his two Gallantry Medals. They shone brightly in the shafts of sunlight coming through the green canopy. Billy heard Owd Isaac earned one of his medals for 'an heroic action on the Somme' and the other one for 'valiant endeavour' on a canal near Nimy, in Belgium. It was also said that Owd Isaac saw the Angel of Mons.

Billy knew all about the Angel of Mons. She was illustrated in one of his dad's three war books, which he kept in the crock cupboard above his armchair to remind him of the war he fought, but didn't talk about, no matter how hard Billy badgered him with questions regarding it. However, his granddad said the Heavenly Event definitely confirmed that God was on the side of the British and the French not the Germans and that was why the War was won.

'Got you,' Owd Isaac suddenly said.

He held up his penknife. An assortment of pipe smoker's aids was attached to it. 'If you're going to be a pipe smoker, lad,' Owd Isaac was saying, 'you should never be without one of these. Indispensable, these are.'

'Oh,' Billy said and wondered what 'indispensable' meant, but decided not to ask after what Owd Isaac said about Curiosity Killing The Cat.

'Oh, aye,' went on Owd Isaac.

The old man began to 'cut-and rub' the tobacco. When he clearly thought he had enough he gathered the fibres together in the hollow of his left hand and then grinned down at him. 'Now then, lad,' he said, 'give us thee pipe.'

Finding it difficult to suppress his excitement, Billy passed the clay over to Owd Isaac. His old friend began to stuff the tobacco into the new bowl. When he was finished he offered the pipe back and said, 'There, stick it in thee mouth and we'll get it lit.'

Billy did as he was bid.

'After we've had a smoke,' Owd Isaac was saying, 'we'll go round and check t' rabbit hangs, to see what we've got.' He grinned down again. 'That's better than going to t' pictures, isn't it, lad?'

'Yeh,' Billy said,

Was it?

Now Owd Isaac produced a shiny chrome cigarette lighter. Expertly, the old man spun the serrated wheel with a grubby thumb. On the second spin the wick ignited. Leaning over towards Billy, he held the lighter over the pipe bowl. The smoking flame hardly flickered in the still evening air.

'Right,' Owd Isaac said, 'begin pulling on her, lad.' Billy began to suck, vigorously, but after a dozen or so puffs the old man said, 'Give her some, lad; you're doing nowt at t' moment.'

Billy began to draw on the pipe even more determinedly. Before long acrid smoke filled his mouth and began rising up to sting his nose and eyes. After more moments he found he needed to pause to cough and splutter, for now the smoke was getting down into his lungs making him feel as though he was suffocating. Pipe tobacco was much stronger than cigarette tobacco. Eventually he found he had to pull the pipe out of his mouth in order to get some air.

Owd Isaac said, 'A bit sharp, is it, lad?'

Billy looked up through dizzy eyes. For a second or two he thought he saw mild humour playing in the old man's wrinkled gaze.

'Yes.'

'A bit different to fags, eh?' Owd Isaac went on.

'Yes,' Billy said.

'You do know you're not lit properly yet, don't you, lad?' Owd Isaac went on. 'And another thing: you're not supposed to swallow t' smoke until you've got used to it. I thought you'd have known that not being a stranger to baccy.'

'It just went down,' Billy said. 'I couldn't stop it.'

Owd Isaac sniffed. 'I see. Well, just take it steady until you get used to it. All right?'

Billy coughed and spluttered some more then said, 'Yeh.'

He put the pipe back into his mouth. Once again the old man leaned over and held the lighter over the pristine bowl. Again Billy began to puff. Soon, clouds of smoke again began to rise. However, it wasn't long before he was barking and spluttering. But this time his convulsions were so violent Owd Isaac held the lighter away from him while he rocked backward and forward coughing and fighting for clean air.

'You're not doing very well, are you, lad?' Owd Isaac said presently.

Something akin to grim determination began to build up in Billy. 'I'll be all right in a minute,' he said. He began to puff with renewed vigour. But now he was beginning to feel really dizzy.

'Are t' sure?' Owd Isaac said.

'Yes.'

'Very well,' said Owd Isaac.

The old man sank back against the hen cote, relit his briar and folded his arms and began to puff. Presently, he sighed. 'This is the life, lad,' he said, contentedly blowing smoke into the air, 'a summer's night, a pipe of baccy and everything at peace with the world. Thou canna buy it, lad. No way.'

Billy gasped, 'C – can't you?' Feelings of nausea were now overwhelming him. He felt as though he was floating. He realised he wanted to be sick, incredibly sick.

'Are t' all right, lad?' Owd Isaac said presently,

But his voice was a faint noise in the distance and Billy shot off the bench, scattering the hens pecking around their feet as he bolted for the nearest tree.

Ignominy came in the form of a spouting flood that splattered against the massive roots of the beech he was bending over. To drive in the final nail of shame, some vomit splashed all over his nearly new

105

Woolworth's pumps.

Owd Isaac's enquiry sounded even more distant 'Are t' all right, lad?'

Billy turned to stare at the old man. He was a blob, swimming against the cote side. The taste in Billy's mouth was foul.

'It must be summat I had for me tea,' he said, after moments.

Owd Isaac raised his brows. 'It's not t' baggy, then?'

'Oh, no,' said Billy. 'Pickles. I had too many pickles. Me mum said they'd make me sick, and they have.'

Owd Isaac said, 'Oh. So it definitely wasn't the tobacco?'

Billy shook his head fervently. 'No.'

Owd Isaac seemed content. 'That's all right then. We wouldn't want to make thee sick, would we?' He heaved a sigh. 'So, are you coming to help me check t' rabbit hangs now you're feeling better? You can finish your pipe as we walk along.'

At the mention of smoking more pigtail twist., Billy immediately felt himself going queasy again. 'I'd better not,' he said, 'I promised me mum I'd be home early.'

Owd Isaac frowned. 'Oh? You didn't say. Well, you'd better be off in that case. We don't want to upset your mum, do we?'

'No.'

Owd Isaac hawked up phlegm and spat it to the ground and looked at him quizzically and said; 'Maybe we'll have another pipe when you're feeling a bit better, eh, lad?'

'Yes,' Billy said.

'It's definitely not t' twist that's put thee off then?'

'Oh, no.'

'Pickles, you said,' Owd Isaac pursued.

'That's right.'

'I'll keep thee pipe here, then, shall I?'

'Yes.'

Billy stumbled off down the wood. He really did feel awful. One thing was for certain; it would be a long time before he smoked pigtail twist again. Maybe he never would. Is that what Owd Isaac wanted?

CHAPTER EIGHT

GHOSTS

October, Billy thought. He was sitting at the table next to the big sash window in the living room. He was eating his marrowbone broth using a spoon as well as occasionally soaking the juices up with pieces from two thick slabs of white Co-op bread near his hand. Sunbeams were shafting in through the glass panes and encasing his curly hair in a light-brown halo.

To Billy October meant shorter days, playing whip-and-top and having conker fights. At present he had a 'tenner' which he unfairly pickled in vinegar and baked in the oven to make it hard. And he loved watching the wind blowing the fallen leaves about causing them to swirl in colourful, crazy flight, down the streets and chase up and down the hills and hollows in Grin Wood occasionally rustling and battering against his face and body when the breeze was strong enough

'Hung himself,' his granddad said. He swept back into place the long flap of grey hair he used to cover his shiny baldpate. It had slipped over his eyes as he forcefully expressed his words.

Billy's granddad was sitting in his big armchair in the corner of the living room. He was staring at Mrs Hence, the Club Woman, with his good eye and his immovable glass eye. Billy knew Mrs Hence was waiting for his mum to come in from doing her housecleaning job down Green Lane and granddad was entertaining her.

She called every week did Mrs Hence to collect the Club Money. His mum and aunty Olive often ordered clothes and things out of the

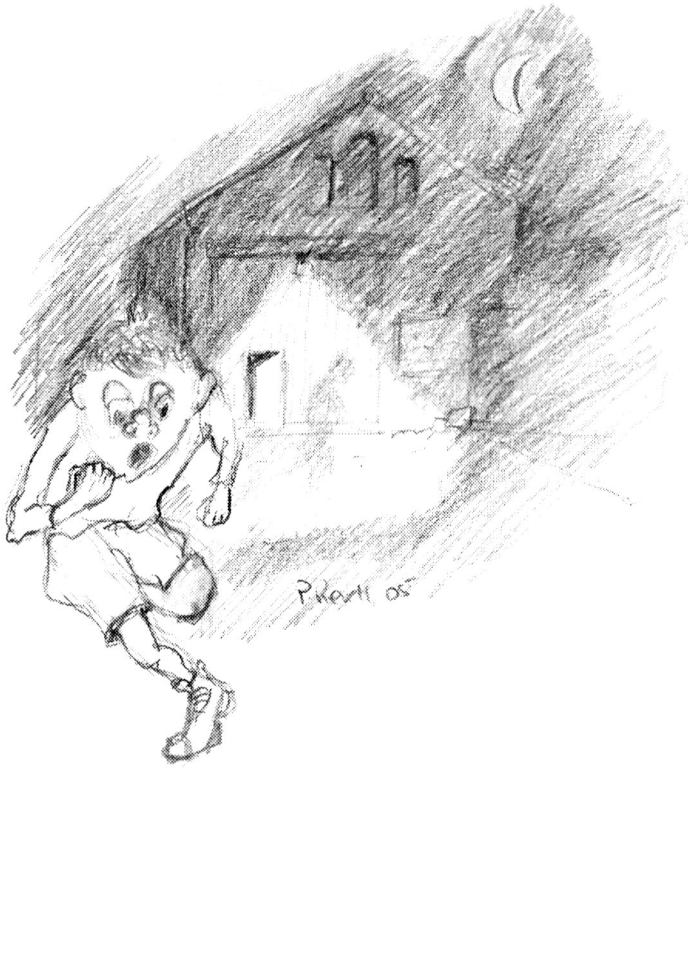

thick book Mrs Hence carried about with her in her big black bag. At the moment the bag was placed beside her on the peg rug covering the front of the cast-iron fender.

As usual Mrs Hence was sitting on the settee sedately drinking the tea his granddad made for her not five minutes ago. She was also nibbling on a digestive biscuit, but when his granddad said, 'Hung himself', she immediately seemed to freeze in mid-motion, the sweetmeat held suspended halfway to her small mouth,

'Who hung himself, Peter?' she said. Her brown eyes were round and alarmed and her breast was already heaving slightly, revealing her concern.

'The coachman,' his granddad said.

'What coachman, for goodness sake?' Mrs Hence said, leaning forward, the biscuit in her hand forgotten.

'It's quite a story,' his granddad went on, 'It happened right where the old Red Lion Inn used to be on Holmfield Road. They call it Lion Cottage now, but then it was a pub. As well as serving ale there, they used to take in the overflow from some of the coach houses down Buxton.'

'Really?' Mrs Hence said, 'I never knew that but it's a farm now.'

'It were then,' said his granddad, 'as well as a pub, but they still took in the overspill. They used to board the driver, passengers and the horn man in little rooms above the coach parks and stables – them places they call the warehouses now. This particular driver I'm talking about actually hung himself in the barn.'

'Good Heavens!' gasped Mrs Hence. 'The hay barn up the yard?'

'No, not that one,' said his granddad. 'This particular barn was pulled down when they built the North Western 'Bus Garage – it's the Derbyshire Stone Garage now, of course.'

'Goodness gracious!' said Mrs Hence. Her eyelids were now open wide.

'Yes,' said his granddad. 'It appears the chap were in all sorts of bother. Strangled his wife, abandoned his children – and, to cap it all, he owed money all over the place. And goodness only knows what else he was wanted for. He was a downright ruffian by all accounts.'

'Heavens above,' exclaimed Mrs Hence, her hand now going to

her heaving, ample breast. 'And this happened in a barn where Derbyshire Stone Garage is now?'

'Yes,' said granddad. 'He hung himself from one of the beams. Climbed up, tied the rope to it and jumped. They say the force of the drop nearly tore his head off. They also say the garage is haunted now.'

'*Haunted*?' said Mrs Hence, her look deeply alarmed. 'Dearie, dearie me; I've never heard anything like it.'

'Oh, aye,' said his granddad, clearly warming to his tale, 'and what's more, the apparition has been seen.'

'By whom?' Mrs Hence gasped.

'Cecil Redfern,' his granddad said.

Billy found his attention was now firmly grasped. He shovelled four tablespoonfuls of the thick marrowbone broth into his mouth in quick succession and then took a bite out of the thick slice of bread he was holding, while gawping awestruck at his granddad. Then he stared at Mrs Hence, to look for any further reaction she would make to the shocking disclosure. The reason he did was because Mrs Hence was usually such a calm woman, even though she always dressed in black, out of deference to her 'dear departed husband, ever missed' who died twelve years ago.

Billy really liked Mrs Hence. She was nice. And she smelled of lavender oil. And she always gave him a large piece of the Palm's Creamy Toffee every time she called for the Club Money. But there was one thing about her that did embarrass him a little. It was the creak her corset stays made when she bent forward to reach her club book. They sounded exactly like Mrs Brier's, his teacher at school when she sat on the edge of the desk near him.

'And I've seen the apparition,' his granddad was saying, 'not very clear mind, but I've seen it.'

'You've actually seen the ghost, Peter?' said Mrs Hence.

'Oh, aye,' said his granddad. 'It was a shadow-like thing. Ominous.'

'Dear, oh, dear,' said Mrs Hence.

Clearly uneasy, she laid her half-drunk cup of tea down on the little table in front of her and placed her half-eaten biscuit down on the plate beside it. While she was doing so, his granddad was gazing up at the ceiling, rubbing his chin, as if ruminating on how he could most fittingly tell the rest of the tale.

'The best way to describe it,' he said presently, 'is to say it was wraith-like.'

'Wraith-like?' echoed Mrs Hence.

'Yes,' said his granddad. 'Weird.'

Billy, found himself now tingling with curiosity. He couldn't hold it in check any longer.

'What does wraith-like mean, granddad?' he said.

His granddad slid his gaze on to him, as if surprised he was listening. 'Ghostly, lad,' he said.

Billy said, 'A proper ghost... over at Derbyshire Stone Garage?'

'Yes,' said his granddad. 'You haven't seen it, have you?'

'No.'

Billy felt fear tipple through him. In order to allay it he gobbled down more broth and more bread. Meantime, his granddad was putting his empty cup and saucer down on the warm hob above the open range. When the task was completed he leaned back in his armchair and clasped his fingers together across his waistcoat and looked gravely at Mrs Hence.

'Cecil Redfern told me he met the apparition once, face to face.'

'*Face to face*?' gasped Mrs Hence. She began fanning her face with an Order Form she lifted out of the capacious black bag by her feet. Her eyes, Billy saw with some concern, now looked really startled. Nevertheless, as if recovering the Club Woman said firmly, 'You must tell me all that happened, Peter, now you've started this.'

His granddad lifted his brows. 'Well, apart from what I've told you, there's nowt else to it really. But Cecil Redfern did emphasise there was an aura of evil about the spectre and that the garage should be avoided at night at all costs.'

Mrs Hence echoed, '*At all costs*?'

'Yes,' his granddad said even more gravely, 'very definitely. Harrumph.'

Mrs Hence looked immensely worried now. 'Oh, my goodness,' she said. Then she added, frowning petulantly and fanning her face, 'I don't know why you felt the need to tell me this, Peter, I really don't. You know how nervous my disposition is since my poor, dear Albert died.'

His granddad sniffed. 'I thought you'd be interested, seeing as you're into Spiritualism and reading Tea Leaves and such like. I didn't think talking about the dead would bother you all that much seeing as you have been in communication with them.'

Mrs Hence sniffed and began playing with the double rope necklace of artificial pearls resting on her black satin covered breast. She looked a little indignant She said, 'Well, I am interested in those things, Peter, but this is not the same thing at all, is it? I mean Spiritualism is more to do with the *ethereal*. It's certainly not about murderers hanging themselves.' Mrs Hence composed herself and went on, 'I go to Meetings because the Medium enables me to keep in touch with my dear Albert. Indeed, I get some very good messages coming through. It's so comforting to me.'

'Oh,' said his granddad. 'I see. I suppose that does alter things a little. Does he still wear his flat cap, your Albert?'

Mrs Hence looked at him severely. "Are you being facetious, Peter?'

'No, I were just wondering.'

Billy was speculating what 'facetious' meant.

Mrs Hence began to waft the Order Form again, 'One thing is for sure, Peter,' she went on, 'I won't be able to pass that place in the dark any more. Particularly now my poor, dear Albert has gone to his rest and cannot escort me.'

Billy saw Mrs Hence's lips begin to tremble. Tears appeared on the edges of her bottom eyelids. She dabbed them with her handkerchief and Billy felt immediate sympathy well up. And, clearly with compassion, his granddad leaned over and took her limp white hand and patted it gently,

'There, there, Nelly lass, don't take on so,' he said. 'Albert's in a far better place, as well you know: safe in the hands of Jesus.'

Mrs Hence seemed to pull herself together. She blew her nose and then said, 'Indeed yes, Peter, that is true. But I do miss him all the same, I really do.'

His granddad patted her hand again. 'Of course you do, lass,' he said, 'It's only natural, but you can't grieve forever.'

'But I do, Peter,' Mrs Hence said, 'I do.'

The chiming grandmother clock standing in the corner behind his granddad's armchair tinged half past five. They were busy up at the sawmill and Billy knew he should be at his stick-chopping-and-bundling job right now.

But he was late because of this hitch that occurred earlier. When he went to collect the Manchester Evening News and the Manchester Evening Chronicle at Buxton LMS station – in order to be able to make up his newspaper round and deliver it – apparently autumn leaves on the line caused the engine to spin its wheels and make the train late. It left Billy wondering as to how such small things as leaves off trees could affect a big snorting monster like a railway engine. It didn't make sense.

He gobbled up the last of his marrowbone broth and got up and looked at Mrs Hence, He wondered where his piece of Palm's Creamy Toffee was. She must have forgotten about it being so upset about her 'dear departed Albert' and the ghost.

He pulled on his jacket, 'I've got to go now, Mrs Hence, so I'll say goodbye,' he said, hoping that would be a good enough hint.

The Clubwoman smiled and stared up at him through tear-wet eyes. 'Oh, yes, goodbye, Billy.' She sighed, but then she held up a hand. 'Oh! Wait a minute.' (*It worked*). She began to rummage in her big black handbag and then lifted out a large white paper bag. 'I almost forgot.'

Beaming his best smile, Billy took the offered confection 'Thanks, Mrs Hence,' he said and then turned and opened the front door, overhearing as he went out, 'He's such a dear boy.' Mrs Hence was saying to his granddad. 'It is my one great regret, Peter, that Albert and me never had children.'

'Aye, I know, lass,' his granddad said. He was patting her hand again. 'And don't worry about the ghost. You only have to ask and I'll escort you home.'

Mrs Hence sniffed. 'Oh, you are kind to me, Peter. It's wonderful to have such friends to fall back on.'

Billy closed the door quietly behind him. A minute later he was racing past Derbyshire Stone Garage. But, as he did, he couldn't help but stare at the huge red doors fronting it. Was there really a ghost haunting the garage, he wondered?

By nine o'clock Billy was standing at the bottom of the road, staring up the hill towards his house. The gas lamp outside the dwelling was casting eerie yellow light through the drifting chill October mist. He shivered in his thin, darned jersey and his short, worn and patched flannel trousers. He should have put his old overcoat on. His mum was always telling him to do so. However, he was never quite sure whether it was going to be cold or not this time of year and he didn't like wearing his overcoat unless he had to.

He stared at the big red doors of the Derbyshire Stone Garage. The small yellow light above them made them look really eerie. Indeed, he hadn't appreciated until now just how frightening the garage could be after dark.

Again he peered at the garage. This time he scanned it thoroughly. He missed nothing. It seemed all right. Then a shadowy shape appeared to drift across the huge red doors and immediately butter-flies stamped across his tummy, it definitely wasn't mist he was staring at.

Now his heart began to thump. His granddad said the apparition took the form of a shadowy shape, drifting across the front of the doors.

Billy set his mind working furiously. He didn't fancy going past the doors now he realised the ghost was there. What he could do was run through the village, across Dolly Peg Row and come in on his home from Over Germany. But that would be admitting he was afraid of the ghost!

He steeled himself, even though his heart was pumping madly against his ribs. He fought his anxiety and took a deep breath and set off up the hill, the muscles of his legs straining as his hobnail boots fought to get the maximum purchase on the tarmac of the pavement. He didn't look at the garage as he went by it; he just kept running, staring at the lamppost ahead using it as if it was some sort of target, or refuge. And in no time at all he found himself swinging on the big stone gatepost of his house and pounding up the concrete path to the front door. Turning the brass knob, he almost fell into the living room. His breath was rasping out of him as he shut the door behind him.

To recover properly he leaned against the overcoats hanging at the back of it.

When he realised he was safe, he looked round. As usual, his granddad was sitting in his armchair in the corner, listening intently to the Nine o'clock News. His dad was reading the Mirror newspaper in the other corner, looking perfectly relaxed. The coal fire glowed in the range grate. Then his mum came in from the kitchen.

'Where've you been?' she said. 'I said be in at half-past eight. It's turned nine. You should've been in bed half an hour ago.'

She paused and looked at him more closely. 'Whatever's the matter with you, child? Have you seen a ghost, or something?'

Billy made for the settee and sat down. He shook his head vigorously, 'No, It weren't there, I beat it.'

His granddad sniffed and coughed and wriggled his eyebrows, then continued listening to the radio, one hand cupped behind his right ear.

'Beat what?' his mum said. 'What on earth are you talking about?'

'The ghost,' Billy said,

'What ghost?'

'Over at the Derbyshire Stone Garage; me granddad said it hung itself.'

His mum turned, her eyes wide and looked at his granddad, 'What have you been filling his head with, father?' she said. She waved a hand at his dad sitting quietly reading in the other armchair. 'I can understand something like that coming from him,' she added, 'but I expect better from you.'

Billy's dad looked over the top of his newspaper and glared. He said, 'It's nowt to do with me.'

His granddad gave out a sigh. 'I wasn't thinking, lass,' he said. 'I got to telling Nellie Hence about that coachman that was supposed to have hung himself across there and the lad must have heard.'

'It's an old wives' tale, and you know it,' his mum said.

His granddad sniffed. 'Oh, I don't know about that, lass. Too many folk claim to have seen it.'

His mum said, 'Well, I've never seen it.' She sighed, 'Well, I can't stand here talking all night, I've got a pile of ironing to do before I can get to my bed.' She turned. 'Right, my lad,' she added, 'I'll get your cocoa, and then I want you up to that bed sharp. And for goodness sake wipe your nose.'

Billy immediately brought his sleeve up.

'Not on your sleeve!'

Billy jumped at the power in his mum's voice and fumbled in his pocket for the piece of old shirt tail she gave him for a handkerchief this morning. Reaching it out he put it to his nose and blew loudly.

Meanwhile, his mother went into the kitchen. Within two minutes she was back with his cocoa and a Marmite butty. Silently, he sipped the cocoa and munched on the sandwich. When he was finished he lighted his candle and muttered goodnight.

The narrow stairs creaked as he climbed them and he made a point of looking for ghosts on the first landing before he climbed the rest of the stairs to the attic. His sister Mary, he found, was fast asleep in her corner alcove.

He yawned vastly and undressed and put on his nightshirt and climbed into the squeaky, iron-frame bed he shared with his brother. He knew his brother wouldn't be home until after eleven o'clock, because he worked at the Spa Cinema down Buxton, operating the projectors. He blew out the candle. The thing was, though, he decided, as he lay back and put his hands behind his head and stared at the pictures the light from the street gas-lamp cast on the ceiling, he had beaten a ghost. How many could say they'd done that?

Outside, an owl hooted.

'Tha can laugh,' he said before drifting into sleep,

CHAPTER NINE

MONICA'S UP TO SUMMAT

Thankfully, over the following week, Billy found the nervousness the ghost created in him was gradually fading. However, since granddad's revelation regarding the spectre, he always passed the Derbyshire Stone Garage with great caution, thoroughly scanning its surrounds before hurrying past – particularly at night.

But now he was walking a lamp and running a lamp down St John's Road, pushing the soapbox handcart he made from bits and pieces begged and bartered for. He was heading for Buxton Station to pick up the late editions of the Manchester Evening News and the Manchester Evening Chronicle,

The newspapers came up on one of the afternoon trains,

As he walked he tried to convince himself he should be tingling with excitement now he and the gang were agreed on what they were going to do tonight. They discussed it in the school playground during afternoon break.

They were going to play Pin and Button. As usual, they were going to meet at seven o'clock around the gas lamp outside the Public Toilets, situated on the triangle across from Christ Church, Burbage. Who the intended victim would be was to be decided when they assembled. However, and this was why he wasn't bubbling with excitement as much as he should have been, there was a fly in the ointment.

It was in the guise of Monica Pane.

She was definitely up to summat.

Once more he paused to turn and stare up the footpath. Monica was still following him, a lamppost distance up from the one he stood by. Why she was shadowing him he didn't know, but it would more than likely lead to trouble in the end. For the last time he heard of Monica Pane following somebody was when she trailed his best pal Wesley Ward to Cavendish Golf Course, when he went looking for golf balls. And look what nearly happened there.

He should ignore her, but he couldn't restrain himself any longer.

'What're you chasing after me for, Pane?' he shouted,

Monica stopped and pouted. 'I'm not. I can walk down St John's Road if I want to. I don't have to ask your permission, Billy Nobstick.'

Billy pointed a grubby finger. 'I'll find out,' he said.

'Find out then,' Monica said, 'and see if I care.'

Billy glared at her. He would dearly like to try to bully an answer out of her, however he didn't like bullying people. In any case, Monica could give as good as she got when she put her mind to it. Nevertheless, there was another more pressing factor in the equation: he needed to collect the newspapers from the station as quickly as he could or he would be in trouble with Mr Belham.

He spurted off down St John's Road, shoving his handcart in front of him. The cart was a good runner. He'd scrapped the wheels and axle off a pram he found abandoned in Grin Wood. He polished up the chrome and lubricated the axle with grease scrounged off a fitter he was friendly with at Derbyshire Stone Garage. Then he screwed them to the bottom of the soapbox he cadged from the manager of the Co-op on Macclesfield Old Road. The bits of timber for the handles he scrounged off his great uncle Vincent, up at Hawberry Farm.

When he got to the LMS station, puffing and panting, he paused and looked behind him. He sighed thankfully. Monica Pane was nowhere in sight. But oddly, at the same time, he felt a slight tug of disappointment. He rather fancied having Monica Pane chasing after him. But that feeling soon passed. He was well rid of her. In the long run, any association with Monica Pane usually turned out to be trouble. Indeed, now feeling a heavy burden was lifted from his shoulders he ran into the Waiting Room and Ticket Office and went straight out on to the Station Platform beyond. The train from Manchester was just pulling in.

Reaching the Parcels Office, he found bundles of hemp-tied newspapers waiting to be picked up. He selected the two bundles marked BELHAM and loaded them into his handcart, then glanced at the crowd milling around him. Indeed, the long platform was alive with noise and movement as people disembarked from the train resting against the buffers at the far end of the platform.

He stared at the engine for a moment. It was like a great, fiery beast, hissing steam and smoke and dripping hot water. Fumes were rising in oily tentacles to the grimy glass arc above, before it escaped through the vent gaps at the apex.

Though he was used to seeing such bustling crowds when it was his turn the fetch the evening papers (he and Piggy Piggott did the job on alternate weeks) they still fascinated him. He simply loved watching people hurrying for the station exits or pausing to buy newspapers, magazines, chocolates or cigarettes from W H Smith's shop – a wooden lock-up cabin pressed against the grimy gritstone wall next to the Waiting Room and Ticket Office.

Amongst the scurrying people he could also see the uniformed porters, their shiny silver watch chains prominent across their black uniform waistcoats. Some were pulling long flat trolleys piled with boxes and goods of all shapes and sizes. Others were employed carrying luggage for smartly dressed ladies and gentlemen, obviously heading for the row of taxis waiting on the rank outside the station doors.

Mingling in with them were businessmen, who, Billy knew – because his granddad told him – worked in Manchester but lived in Buxton. They were probably hurrying off to their homes around The Park, or on St John's Road; or Green Lane, or Macclesfield Road, or some other posh area around the town.

Though he was exhilarated by the frantic energy of it all, Billy reluctantly turned to the job he was here to do. Eagerly shoving his cart along the platform, deftly swerving it around the porters and passengers, he emerged into the bright autumn sunlight beyond the Waiting Room and Ticket Office doors. Soon he was running along the gritstone-flagged footpath towards Station Approach. But he came to an abrupt halt when, not twenty yards on, he saw Monica Pane leaning with her back against the wall. To make matters even worse, she was smiling. Monica Pane hardly ever smiled... at him anyway.

'Can I help you, Billy?' she said.

'To do what?'

'Push the trolley.'

'It's a cart.'

'Cart, then.'

'No.'

Monica's smile faded and she pouted, her brow now creasing with unhappiness. 'Why not?'

'Because you're up to summat,' Billy said.

'No, I'm not.'

'Yes, you are.'

'Why should I be up to something?' Monica demanded.

'Because you wouldn't be here if you weren't,' Billy said, 'You always say you don't like me – so you must be up to summat.'

'I like you sometimes,' Monica said.

'Oh, aye?' Billy took pains to emphasise his doubt and began to manoeuvre the handcart past her. However, she immediately turned and started to skip along beside him – smiling again.

He stopped abruptly. 'I said you couldn't come, Pane. Are you deaf, or summat?'

'No you didn't,' Monica said, 'you said I couldn't push the cart.'

'I meant both,' Billy said.

Monica pouted. 'You should say what you mean then.'

Now mumbling darkly Billy began pushing the handcart along the footpath. When he got to the end of the gritstone flags he sprinted across the bottom of Palace Road and then scampered down Station Approach. However, Monica still skipped along beside him. Billy now blushed. It was dawning on him. If any of the gang saw him with Monica Pane in tow – or worse, if Piggy Piggot's lot saw him – he would never live it down. No real boy wanted to be seen alone with a sissy girl.

To try and shake her off he scampered post the Devonshire Royal

Hospital. However, Monica easily tripped along beside him on her black, patent leather shoes, her cupid-bow lips still curved into a sweet smile, her blue eyes gazing at him with what appeared to be unadorned admiration. No, he read that wrong. Admiration? It couldn't possibly be… could it?

Monica suddenly took hold of the left hand handle of his cart, her fingers closing gently over his. The contact was like an electric shock. He pulled his hand away as though stung, 'Hey up, what d'you think you're playing at?' he said.

Her gaze was a picture of sweet innocence. 'I really *do* want to help you. Billy.'

He glared. 'I told you no.'

The happiness faded from her eyes.

'But why not. Billy?'

'Because you're up to summat, I said. How many times do you want telling?'

Monica now looked even unhappier. 'I'm not,' she said. Then her voice almost pleaded, 'Oh, go on, Billy. Please.'

The hapless look in her blue eyes became almost unbearable to Billy and an odd feeling of guilt spread through him. Why, he didn't know. However, he found himself allowing her hand to stay where it was. Indeed, he felt slightly flattered by the fact that Monica Pane wanted to hold her hand over his. But, what became more disturbing, Monica began stroking his fingers.

'I think you're ever so nice. Billy,' she said. 'D' you think I'm nice?'

Billy stared, almost lost for words. 'Eh?'

Monica batted her eyelids. 'D' you think I'm nice?'

'I - I've never thought about it.'

Monica smiled. 'Oh, yes you have. I've seen you looking at me.'

Billy felt heat flush up into his face.

'Why should I look at thee?' he said. 'You're nowt special.'

He knew he lied.

He put his head down and began pushing the cart furiously along the path. Monica kept pace. He found he was so affected by Monica's behaviour he nearly hit a lamppost in his effort to get away, Only at the last split-second did he manage to steer round it. Abruptly now, as though stroking his hand wasn't enough for her, Monica reached up and began to stroke his curly nut-brown hair.

'I love your curls, Billy,' she said.

That really incensed him. 'Leave off, will you?'

But it was as if she didn't hear him.

'It's so soft and wavy,' she said, 'Do you eat up your crusts?'

'Eh?' he said, feigning ignorance. But he knew if he ate his crusts his hair would curl. His mum told him. That was why he usually avoided eating his crusts. He didn't want soppy curly hair! He wanted to brush it straight back like Tarzan.

Monica shook out her own tresses and looked at him.

'Do you like my hair?' she said.

He stared at her auburn ringlets, spiralling down from under her blue beret. 'It's all right, I suppose.'

'Me mum did it with the curlers last night,' Monica said.

'Oh?' Who was interested in that, Billy wondered?

Monica said, 'Me mum said hair is a woman's crowning glory and she should wash and comb it every day until it shines.'

Billy stared. 'Every day?'

'Yes,' Monica said. 'At least.'

'At least.'

'Yes.'

Billy found that even harder to believe. His hair was lucky if it saw a comb once a week. Even then his mum usually did it for him while she scolded him about him being such an untidy little wretch.

But now, totally embarrassed by such soppy talk, he started to look around him for some means of escape – some excuse that would enable him to break away from the problem of having Monica Pane walking with him and constantly embarrassing him.

They were passing the nice bungalow next to the Serpentine when he spotted the other thing he was dreading – next to meeting Piggy Piggott's lot, that is. Winker Benton.

Winker was sitting on the seat that went round the big beech tree, situated at the head of Gadley Lane. He appeared to be inspecting some conkers in his lap. As soon as he spotted him, Winker put the conkers in his pocket, got up and leered down the road at him. When he got close Winker said,

'H - hey up. Billy, you n - never t - tell anybody, d - do you?'

Monica Pane giggled.

'Tell anybody what?' Billy said.

Winker smirked and wagged a finger. 'Thee and M - Monica.'

As if in astonishment Billy pointed to Monica and then himself. '*Me, going out with her*?' he said. 'You must be barmy.'

Monica's giggling instantly stopped. 'Why what's wrong with me?'

'Nowt,' Billy said, 'but we aren't going out together, are we? You just offered to help push me cart and that were it, weren't it?'

Monica stamped her patent-leather-clad right foot and looked as though she was going to burst into tears at any moment

'You're horrible you are. Billy Nobstick,' she said. 'What's wrong with going out with me?'

'Nowt,' Billy said, 'if we we're going out. But you just latched on, didn't you? I'll say it again: you're up to summat.'

Monica began to cry. Anxiously Billy looked about him to see if there was anybody about. Sure enough, the relief road sweeper, Mr Madely – the regular one being on holiday – popped his head around the other side of the huge beech tree. Mr Madely was holding the Racing Times in his hand. Making matters worse, Billy knew the Madely family was very friendly with the Pane family – so friendly they were in each other's pockets,

'Now then, what's going on?' Mr Madely said. He looked intently at Monica. 'Are these two bothering thee, lass?'

Monica wailed even more loudly.

Mr Madely turned to Billy, his grey stare stern. 'What have you been saying to her?'

Billy glowered resentfully, 'Nowt.'

'A - aye, n - nowt.' Winker joined in, even though Billy knew Winker didn't have the foggiest idea what this was all about. But there was this unwritten code: the gang stuck together, no matter what the problem was.

'Then why is she crying?' Mr Madely was saying.

Billy shrugged. 'I don't know. Ask her.'

'Monica?' Mr Madely said.

Monica simpered behind her hands. 'I was only trying to help Billy push his cart,' she said.

'I didn't ask her to,' Billy said.

Monica wailed even more loudly and, clearly concerned, Mr Madely went to her side and placed his right arm around her slim shoulders. 'There, there, Monica love,' he said, and then further advised, 'Just keep away from them. You know your mother doesn't like you mixing with them. They're nowt but trouble that lot, most of t' time.'

'No, we're not,' said Billy, his resentment rampant.

'N - no way,' said Winker, equably indignant 'There's n - nowt wrong w - with us.'

That brought an even greater howl from Monica and it seemed to incense Mr Madely. He turned and waved his besom at them.

'Just clear off,' he said.

The brush came close enough to cause Billy to jump back, 'Hey up,' he howled. 'You nearly hit me.' And instantly, Monica stopped crying. Billy saw her blue eyes were now peering over the horizon of her hands. Her face was dry – no tears at all. 'Look at her,' he protested, 'she's just putting it on.'

Mr Madely turned and stared at Monica. She quickly buried her head into her hands and began blubbering again and Mr Madely turned to them. 'It doesn't look like that to me,' he said; 'she looks really upset to me.'

He began to wave the besom again. 'Now just clear off, or I'll clatter you with this.'

'Well, that suits me,' Billy said. 'I don't want her hanging round.'

'N - nor me,' Winker said.

It was almost with glee that Billy once more started pushing his cart up St John's Road. Whatever Monica's motives were for hanging around him and embarrassing him didn't seem to matter in the least now. Even so, he would have liked to know what she was really up to...

Winker walked with him. He fished out his conkers from his pocket. He began throwing the smallest unwanted ones at a fat black and white cat that was leisurely ambling across the road. Typically, he missed each time.

Presently he said, 'W - what was a - all t - that with M - Monica, Billy?'

Billy shrugged. 'Nowt. She followed me down to the station. I tried to shake her off but she wouldn't go.'

'L - looks to me as t - though she's up to s - summat,' Winker said.

'That's exactly what I thought,' Billy said.

'S - she's always up to s - summat is M - Monica Pane,' Winker went on, as if he knew her wiles intimately, which. Billy knew, he didn't. Winker always seemed to be on the periphery of everything, never quite fully involved. Like feasting on the fortunes, or misfortunes, of others.

They were approaching the lane that led down to Otterhole Farm, when Billy decided to glance back to confirm he really was free of Monica Pane. To his horror, she was only four yards behind him.

'I said to clear off!' he shouted.

Monica stuck her nose in the air.

'I can walk up St John's Road if I want to.'

Mr Madely called, 'I told you to keep away from them, Monica. Have I been talking to myself?'

'It's all right, Mr Madely,' Monica said. 'Billy's just apologised to me.' She smiled. 'Haven't you. Billy?'

Billy stared, once more lost for words in the face of such rank dishonesty. 'Eh?'

Mr Madely called, with a sigh, 'Well, I've done my best.'

He clearly wanted to wash his hands of the whole thing. He turned and started collecting up piles of dead leaves with two boards and putting them into his wheelbarrow. It was fitted with temporary high sides to accommodate the abundance of leaves the autumn season produced.

When they got to the ginnel joining St John's Road with Macclesfield Road, Winker halted. 'Right, I'm o - off for me t - tea now, pal,' he said, 'I'll see you r - round the l - lamppost near the t - toilets at s - seven o'clock.'

Billy nodded, 'And don't be late. We want a good start.'

'I - it won't be m - me that you'll be w - waiting for,' Winker said, 'it'll more l - likely be H - Hump Bramble.'

'Can't argue with that,' Billy said.

As Winker went running up the ginnel Billy felt Monica's hand rest on his arm. 'We're alone again. Billy,' she said,

Billy groaned and began furiously walking up the road. It became clear Monica was, again, not to be outdone. She skipped merrily along beside him, smiling at him even more radiantly. Billy increased his pace, but Monica skipped on, easily matching his stride with her long, skinny legs. When they got to Mr Belham's shop Monica said, 'You and the gang are playing Pin and Button tonight, aren't you. Billy?'

Billy felt fully vindicated. 'So you are up to summat,' he said.

'I heard you talking in the playground,' she said, 'Oh, please. Billy, I've never been Pin and Buttoning.'

'No way,' Billy said. 'Anyway, it won't be up to me, it'll be up to t' gang.'

'You can talk to them,' Monica said.

'No, I can't,' Billy said. 'They won't take any notice of me. I'm just one of t' gang, same as them. Everything goes on what we agree together.'

Monica lifted her chin defiantly. 'Well, it doesn't matter because I know exactly where you're going to meet. I heard Dennis Benton telling you just now. I can be there like the rest of you. You can't stop me being at the lamp at seven o'clock.'

'They won't let you play,' Billy said.

'I'll just follow you, then,' said Monica defiantly.

At that moment Mr Belham came to the door of his lock-up shop. The usual Park Drive cigarette was hanging from the corner of his mouth and his black trilby hat was pushed back off his forehead, exposing half of his white baldpate. 'Now, Billy lad, come on,' he said, 'you'll have t'night.' He formed a half-grin, 'You can do thee courting later.'

'I'm not courting?' Billy said resentfully.

Monica giggled behind her hand and Mr Belham said, 'Aye, all right, lad, whatever tha says. All I require you to do is to get those papers in here as quick as you can so we can get 'em sorted and delivered.'

Piggy Piggott came to the lock-up shop doorway and leaned on the jamb. He smirked, 'Tha never said, Billy.'

Billy glared. 'Before tha starts there's nowt to it.'

Piggy chortled. 'Course there isn't. Ha, ha, ha.'

Billy glared. 'Nowt, dost hear?'

Monica said, sweetly. 'I'll see you tonight. Billy.' She gave him her most gushing smile and sparkling wave before she went skipping off up the road, clearly as pleased as Punch.

'Bye, bye. Billy,' mimicked Piggy in his best squeaky voice.

Billy clenched his fists. 'Tha'd better shut thee gob, Piggott,' he said. 'Else I'll be starting summat.'

'Thee and whose army?' Piggy jeered.

'I won't need an army,' Billy said.

Piggy sniggered and began singing, 'Only a rose, I bring you.'

'Thou's asking for it,' Billy said.

'Now shut up you two and get in here, or I'll be putting some advertisements in t' paper,' said Mr Belham.

With that threat they both complied, with alacrity.

The church clock was striking seven. Billy stared round at the faces of the gang gathered under the pool of yellow light shed by the gas lamp they were standing under – at the point where St John's Road met Macclesfield Rood. Monica Pane was standing next to him, her round cheeks rosy. She'd just arrived, to the consternation of all. Billy noted she was fully protected against the chill. She was wearing a big red woolly beret, a long green woolly coat. Her long, spindly legs were clad in thick, black woollen stockings and on her feet were brown lace-up boots. Clearly having waited for the booming chimes of the church clock to finish Wesley Ward now said, 'What d' you want, Pane?'

'Billy said I could come,' said Monica.

Billy reared up. 'No I didn't. I said it weren't up to me.'

Winker Benton said, 'She's b - been mithering B - Billy ever since he c - come out of s- school.'

'Well, we're not having her hanging about and that's final,' Wesley declared. He looked at the faces of the gang. 'Right?'

Eddie Green said, 'Aye, Pin and Button's not a girl's game.'

Hump Bramble said, 'Does your mother know you're out, Monica?'

'She thinks I'm at Shirley Grimshaw's.'

'W - well, if s - she does come,' Winker said, 'it'll be nowt to d - do w - with us if she g - gets caught, will it?' He looked round at the ring of faces, illuminated by the gas lamp. 'It'll be of her o - own doing, w - won't it? I m - mean, w - we're not going to g - get blamed for her, are we?'

'No way,' said Hump Bramble.

Monica put her nose higher in the air, 'Well, I'm not bothered. I can run as fast as any of you lot. It won't be me that'll be caught.'

Billy said, 'Well, we'll have to decide summat. We can't stand here all night. I say let her come if she wants to, as long as she fends for herself.'

Percy Green said, grumpily, 'We should vote on it.'

'All right,' Billy said, 'I say yes, because she'll only hang round whether we say yes or no. One thing's for sure; while we stand here arguing, we'll get nowt done.'

Wesley nodded, 'On the face of that I'm with Billy.'

Hump Bramble said, 'My bet is if she gets caught, she tells on us straight away. That's how girls are. She'll get us all into a bother.'

Monica stamped her foot. 'No, I won't,' she said fiercely. She pointed her woollen-gloved finger. 'It'll be you more like, Timothy Bramble.'

'W - well it's n - no use us s - standing here,' said Winker, 'are w - we letting her come, or a - aren't we?'

On a sudden impulse – Billy knew he could be like that and usually regretted it later – he said, "Oh, I'll look out for her if that's what's going to hold us up.'

Wesley nudged him and warned, 'Don't do it, pal.'

Billy shrugged. 'Somebody's got to. She's made up her mind, that's plain.' He turned and stared at Monica. 'But you'd better do as you're told. I don't want any mucking about if we run into trouble.'

Monica's eyes shone, almost with adoration. 'I will, Billy,' she said, 'honest.'

'You'd better,' Billy snorted. He stared round at the gang. 'Does that settle it then?'

Hump Bramble shrugged. 'It's up to you, pal,' he said indifferently.

They were making their way up Duke Street when Monica said, 'Which house are we going to do?'

'Listen to her,' said Wesley. 'Which house are we going to do?' he mimicked. 'You'd think she knows all there was to know.'

Hump Bramble, obviously not bothered either way now no responsibility rested on him, said, 'How about wotshisname on Green Lane? Him as always comes out and has a go at us.'

'Hey, yeh,' said Percy Green eagerly. 'He's always good for a laugh.'

'Right,' said Billy, 'it's him, then.' He rubbed his hands together in anticipatory delight.

They arrived at the big detached house. Billy saw there were lights on in the large front room. The light from them was casting yellow slivers of luminance through the tiny gaps in the heavy, drawn curtains on to the rose beds. The window was a big, cream painted bay. Billy knew there was plenty of good wood in the frames to stick a drawing pin in. Acute excitement began to build in him. He grinned at the pale faces around him in the misty gloom. Each faint visage, he saw, was alive with excitement and anticipation. Billy took a deep breath to quell his own elation, for it was his responsibility to stick in the pin. He saw no point in waiting,

'Right,' he said. 'Are we ready?'

'Yeh,' said Eddie Green, grinning.

'Shall I come with you, Billy?' Monica said.

He frowned at her. 'Not likely; you stay here with the others.'

With that he crept down the long limestone gravel drive to the bowed window. He was the acknowledged expert at fixing pins and buttons to window frames, though Wesley always claimed it was that way because the rest of them were too scared to do it. But disclaiming that, Hump Bramble began trailing along behind him.

Billy stopped. 'Hey up,' he hissed.

'It's my pin and button,' said Hump resentfully.

Billy shrugged, 'Suit yourself.'

Reaching the window Billy pressed his face against the window and glimpsed through the slight gaps in the curtains. He could see the victim and his wife were sitting in their comfortable armchairs, one each side of the cheerfully burning coal fire. Using the fans of radiance coming from the two electric standard lamps, the man was reading a book, the woman a magazine.

With a conspiratorial look on his face, Hump grinned across at Billy and pulled the pin, button and cotton reel out of his trouser pocket. Billy was pleased to see the pin and button was already prepared. The arrangement of the apparatus was very simple. Tie a short length of thread from the long-stemmed drawing pin to the button, and then fasten the yards of thread on the full bobbin to the middle of the joined pin and button. Thus prepared it allowed the operator to swing the button back and forth against the window producing a monotonous, annoying rattle.

Hump shoved the equipment towards him. Billy took them. He would need to stand on tiptoe to stick the pin into the upper crosspiece of the bow window, but that was not a hardship.

The pin firmly secured he carefully lowered the thread with the button attached to it so it hung down near the large, polished glass pane below. Then he turned to Hump who was holding the bobbin of cotton thread, attached to the middle of the down piece between the pin and the button. He was meticulous in keeping the button off the window by holding it away with the bobbin thread. Now hardly daring to breathe, he made his way back up the drive Hump tiptoeing ahead of him.

Back with the rest of the gang Billy crouched down behind the house's garden fence, which smelled strongly of creosote. The misty October night was eerie. But he didn't think of ghosts. Another kind of excitement consumed him.

Before he started, he gazed around him. Where was Monica? He needed to know her exact position for when they needed to make a run for it, for they would surely have to with this chap. She was behind the left gatepost, leaning forward, eagerly peering through the bars of the green-and-cream-painted double gates. She was obviously waiting for the fun to start.

Tingling with excitement he commenced working the thread. Soon the all too familiar sound of button meeting glass came with monotonous regularity.

Tap, tap, and tap. Tap, tap, and tap.

Surprising them all, within two minutes, the front door of the house burst open and the owner came scurrying out in running shorts and singlet. He made straight for the position where the pin and button was fixed. Billy jerked the pin out of the wood and feverishly wound in the cotton thread and pocketed it while the man fumbled all over the window, trying to find it

Somebody yelled, 'Blinking heck, he means it this time!'

The scatter was instant. Billy grabbed Monica's warm gloved hand.

'Come on, or he'll have us?'

Monica momentarily hesitated, exhilaration shining on her face, and then took off like a gazelle and Billy found he needed to put on an extra spurt to keep up with her. The odd thing was Monica was giggling with apparent delight.

At the lane that went down the back of Duke Street Billy said, 'Down there, quick.'

Monica obeyed. But all the time Billy was anxiously thinking. He must do something about Monica, She was supposed to be at Shirley Grimshaw's. And she was supposed to be a nice girl from a good family and didn't get into any trouble of any sort – especially with boys.

He remembered there was a big open-fronted garage three quarters of the way down the lane. The owner had an open sided lorry parked inside it. Billy thought it would make the perfect hideaway for Monica while he led their pursuer off. He quickly steered Monica into its dark maw.

'Stay in here,' he hissed. 'When I've drawn him off, run straight home and don't say nowt to anybody, d' you hear?'

Monica was staring at him round-eyed, but clearly still exuberantly excited. 'Yes, Billy,' she said.

'I'm serious.'

'I know.'

With that he galloped off down the lane. Where it made a left angle to turn on to Duke Street Billy stopped and turned. Soon he made out the man's white singlet and shorts as he came trotting towards him through the misty gloom. His excitement winding up to fever pitch Billy stepped out and jumped up and down, waving his arms and blowing raspberries.

'I'm here,' he shouted, 'I'm here!'

The man stopped for a moment and then began sprinting again; straight for him. Billy scooted off round the bend. Soon he was on to Duke Street. He hurried down past the Duke of York, down Nursery Lane, and on through the gap between the Band Room and the Institute, then across the Bowling Green, over the wall and then he burrowed into a pile of wood and leaves that had been collected under the wall. He had used the hideout before. He waited, trying to shallow his breathing. Not bothering about the mouse that came to have a look at him.

He heard the man searching around the Band Room, and then the Institute, His noises gradually came nearer. Suddenly the man shouted, 'I know where you are.'

Billy squeezed himself into an even tighter ball and closed his eyes and waited, making himself ready to bolt should he need to. But gradually the din of the search faded away into the distance. Soon after the church clock sombrely struck nine. A different kind of alarm coursed through Billy now.

He was supposed to be in the house for half past eight!

He wriggled out of his hiding place and crept along in the cover of the moss-covered wall that separated the church graveyard from Backhouse's Field. Coming to the corner of the churchyard he slithered over the wall, scampered up the pasture and clambered over the five-barred gate by the Co-op Shop. Then he ran along Macclesfield Old Road and up the ginnel on to Leek Road.

When he got into the house, as usual, his dad was sitting in one corner near the fireplace. He was reading the Manchester Evening Chronicle. His granddad was sitting in the other corner He was listening to the Nine o'clock News on the wireless. His vein-seamed right hand was cupped to his hairy ear. Billy could hear his mum busy in the kitchen. His dad rustled the newspaper and looked up.

'Where hast thee been?'

'Hump Bramble's, making a jigsaw. Their clock stopped and his mother's washing up at the Spa Hotel, so we didn't know what time it was.'

His dad didn't look convinced. 'Is that t' best tha can do?'

It was at that moment his mum came in from the kitchen. Immediately, she pointed to the ceiling,

'Up,' she ordered.

Billy pulled his best pleading face. 'But I've had no supper.'

'Up.'

'It's not fair.'

'Up.'

In bed, in the attic, and in just his shirt. Billy mumbled to himself about the injustice of it all and then blew out the candle and stared at the pictures the shadows from the gas lamp outside made on the ceiling.

Slowly, he calmed down. Even though he was very hungry, the tingle of the evening's adventure still warmed him. He wondered if Monica Pane got home all right, if the gang did, or if the man chasing him recognised him.

He heard the whisper of carpet slippers on the stairs and then his mum came quietly into the attic. 'It's a cheese sandwich,' she said, as she came close. She smelt of lavender.

'Mind you don't make any crumbs.'

She gave the butty to him, smoothed and patted his forehead before going quietly out of the room and down the stairs.

Different warmth filled Billy now. He settled down under the bed-clothes and took a big bite out of the sandwich. He wondered again if Monica Pane had got home all right. She must have done, he decided. But why should he be worried about Monica Pane? She was nowt but trouble.

Smiling, he stuffed the rest of the sandwich into his mouth and snuggled down. A fox was making a din somewhere in Grin Wood and he wondered if Owd Isaac's hens were all right.

P Revill 05

CHAPTER TEN

BUNNIES AND VEGETARIANS

To Billy, as he gazed at the lowering sky racing across the top of Burbage Edge, it didn't seem a fortnight had passed since the Pin and Button episode. But he did notice the days were getting shorter and the air cooler.

Monica Pane told him – the day after the chase – she did get safely home. Now she was back, sometimes putting her tongue out at him and giggling with her friends, but most of the time she was just generally ignoring him. She didn't even thank him for rescuing her, not that it bothered him. In fact, it suited him down to the ground if it kept her away from him. Girls in general, he decided, and Monica Pane in particular, were more trouble than they were worth.

But the thing that was really important to him at this moment was the idea that came to him during morning playtime – to go rabbit hunting with the gang. They'd never been on a rabbit hunt together and he was instantly gratified to hear nearly everyone was keen on the idea.

As for killing the rabbits… well, he had no qualms about that. Owd Isaac showed him how to kill rabbits over a year ago.

The recollection was still vivid.

They found this rabbit still alive in one of Owd Isaac's hangs, caught by one of its hind legs. Owd Isaac freed it and held it up by its back legs. Triumph was in his eyes, 'He's a grand un, lad,' he said. He looked down at him, quizzically. 'Have you ever killed a rabbit before?'

Billy shook his head.

Owd Isaac said, 'Well, there's nowt to it. All you have to do is owd it up like I'm doing now and hit it at t' back of its ears – a sharp chop down with the edge of your hand. Like this.'

The old man sliced down with his blue-veined hand, just as though he was chopping with an axe, but he stopped short of the rabbit's neck,

'Like that,' he said. 'Hast got it?'

'I think so,' Billy said,

'So, how about it?'

'How about what?'

'Killing it.'

Butterflies did a clog dance in Billy's stomach. 'Me?'

Owd Isaac nodded, his bushy brows wobbling. 'Who dost think I mean? You've got to start somewhere, lad. It's good meat is rabbit and if you catch one you'll have to know how to kill it.'

'I suppose so,' Billy said.

At the prospect of killing a rabbit. Billy found that his heart was beginning to thump. His throat was also becoming as dry as a bone, making it hard to swallow. But the notion of actually having to kill something created deep curiosity in his mind. Not only that there was this primitive instinct impelling him irresistibly towards the idea of taking life for food. Nevertheless, he found there was something repulsive about it.

'Couldn't I practice on summat first?' he said.

Owd Isaac again raised his bushy, greying brows. 'Practice?' he said. 'Nay, lad, it's got to be done for real; first time; no messing about.'

'But...'

'No buts, either,' Owd Isaac said firmly. He thrust out the struggling rabbit. 'Here, take hold of it. It's nowt but the way of nature.'

Billy realised his heart was now really pounding.

'But...'

Owd Isaac raised a hand. 'What did I say?'

Reluctantly, Billy took the rabbit and held it up by its hind legs –

almost at arm's length. It was still bobbing and jerking about and making strange snorting noises. Billy found his heart was running like a trip-hammer now, enough to cause blood to drum in his ears, like seawater thrashing against shale.

'Kill it now?' he said.

'Get on with it,' said Owd Isaac. 'Don't keep the poor beggar in suspense. That's the worst thing tha can do. It's cruel. I don't hold with cruelty. If it's got to be done, do it as humanely and as quickly as possible. Just think of it as meat, lad. Your dinner for tomorrow if you like.'

Billy stared at the nape of the rabbit's neck. The fur was light brown. He swallowed once again on his dry throat. He was going to kill a living thing. The thought began to take on awesome complexities. Nevertheless, he steeled himself, took a deep breath and brought the edge of his hand down as hard as he could. If he had to do it, then he would make it as quick a possible like Owd Isaac advised him to do.

The blow connected with force on the rabbit's neck, right where Owd Isaac indicated it should be hit and the animal instantly stopped jerking and stiffened. Urine leaked out from under its white tail and it went limp.

Though awed by the act of destruction he had just committed. Billy became aware Owd Isaac was beaming down at him and patting him on the shoulder. 'There, what did I tell you?' he was saying. 'Nowt to it. That were just perfect, lad. Thou art a natural; if I ever saw one; it never felt a thing.'

Billy stared. 'How d' you know it didn't?'

'I'd bet a pound on it,' said Owd Isaac. 'Clean as a whistle, that was.'

Billy felt pride flushing through him. 'I only give it one smack,' he said.

'And that were more than enough, lad,' Owd Isaac enthused. 'Now then, seeing as you've killed it, tha'd better take it home with you. I'm sure your mum'll make a right good pie out of that one – enough to feed all of thee.'

Billy, wide-eyed, said, 'D'you mean it?'

'Of course I mean it,' said Owd Isaac. 'I wouldn't say it if I didn't mean it, would I?'

'No,' Billy said.

'So, there you are then,' said Owd Isaac.

But in the playground that afternoon Billy found there was one who had reservations about the hunt

'It's poaching,' Hump Bramble said. 'We'll get caught.'

'Are you scared?' Wesley Ward said,

Hump glared. 'No,' he said. He hesitated, then. 'It's me mum; she doesn't like people killing things.'

'It won't be thee mum doing it,' Billy said.

Eddie Green said, 'And since when have you bothered about what your mum says, Bramble?'

'A - aye,' stammered Winker Benton fervently, 'since w - when?'

Hump Bramble glared at them and then sulkily kicked sparks off the tarmac playground with his boot studs.

So here they were at six o'clock, near the top of Burbage Edge. In the misty, pearl-grey evening light Billy gazed around him. The gang was all here, but Hump Bramble was still moaning.

Billy fumbled with the sack containing Owd Isaac's snaring nets. He ran up to his old friend's hut after school and borrowed them. While he did he gazed along the bare length of the old Cromford and High Peak Railroad track towards Tunnel Farm, not visible in the misty distance. The iron road was taken up long ago when the barge trade failed, so his granddad once told him.

Billy took a deep breath. He loved the damp, peaty smell of the moor at this time of year. It was pungent and exhilarating. Then he swivelled his gaze to the rabbit warren. It was in the field to his left. The reed clotted pasture sloped up to the trees along the top of the Edge. He could see dozens of rabbits bobbing in and out of their holes, eating grass and enjoying the last of the day.

'We'll get caught,' Hump Bramble said once more. 'We should've gone to Big Bushy and baked some spuds.' He began to beat his hands across his chest. 'And it's flipping cold up here. Another thing:

nobody knows owt about snaring rabbits. And nobody knows how to kill them.'

'I do,' Billy said.

'And me,' said Wesley. 'Me dad showed me.'

'Even so, it's still poaching,' Hump said. Farmers don't like people poaching on their land.'

Wesley Ward said, 'Just shut your gob, will you. Bramble? You've done nowt but moan since Billy mentioned it this afternoon.'

But Hump continued. 'Owd whatshisname, him over the hill as owns the land; he'll be along any minute, you see.' He glowered around him. 'Anyway, what was to stop us going rabbitting up in Grin Wood? There are plenty of rabbits in there and nobody'll bother us in there.'

Billy said, 'No way, Owd Isaac works Grin Wood, I'm not letting anybody tread on his corns. In any case, if somebody does come along from t' farm we'll be able see them a mile off.'

'Yeh,' said Eddie Green. 'So shurrup, Bramble.'

Hump looked away and sulked.

Billy turned to Wesley. In the sack his friend was carrying was Wesley's dad's ferret. Wesley's dad called the animal Beauty. Billy didn't know why because it was a right vicious little brute,

Hump, looking uncertain, said, 'Can you handle that ferret, Wardy?'

Wesley glared. 'Course I can.'

'Suppose it doesn't come out of t' hole; what shall you do then, eh,' Hump continued to moan.

'It will,' said Wesley and glared. 'Now then, is there owt else you want a bloody moan about?'

'Aw, just ignore him,' Billy said.

'A - aye,' Winker Benton said. 'I - ignore him.'

Billy emptied the dozen nets Owd Isaac lent to him out of the sack. They tumbled on to the cinders of the track. He gathered them up.

'Right,' he said, looking round at the rest of the gang, 'let's get on with it, or we'll have it dark.'

Agreement came, except from Hump.

Billy hopped over the wall. The rabbits scattered, ears back, into their holes, white tails flashing bright in the dull light. Billy scrambled up the field to the warren and began to set out his stall; putting nets over the holes.

The gang followed him round, asking if they could do anything. Hump Bramble, though, moved a little further up the hill and stood watching them. After moments he called, 'It won't work.'

Billy stared daggers at him. 'Look, if you want something to do, go higher up the hill and keep a look out.'

'Aye,' said Winker Benton, 'm - make thee self u - useful.'

'You won't catch a ruddy thing, I tell thee.' Hump trudged up the hill adding as he went, 'Nowt. Not a sausage.'

Percy Green looked around. 'What the flipping heck is up with him?'

Wesley Ward said, 'Sod him, the miserable bugger.'

He opened the Hessian bag he was carrying and lifted out Beauty. She was yellow and lithesome and fearsome-looking, and when she emerged she stared at Billy with orange eyes. Billy stared back resentfully. He still had a scab on his index finger, a memento from his last encounter with Beauty. Wesley asked him to hold the animal while he made a gap in the boarding around the bottom of Welmet's hen cote so he could put the ferret in to flush out the rats that were eating all Mr Welmet's eggs. It was then the ratty little thing bit him.

Wesley petted the beast lovingly. 'Now then,' he said in its ear, 'let's see what you're made of and put it down the hole.'

The gang scattered – as Billy explained they should do earlier – to take up their positions over their respective nets. Crouched over his, Billy waited, excitement slowly beginning to build up in him. For quite some time nothing happened then squealing came from below.

Billy yelled, 'Hey up, they'll be coming in a minute.'

Soon, all over the warren, rabbits began erupting out of holes to become enmeshed in the nets.

Almost immediately Winker Benton yelled, 'I've g - got one!'

'Neck it,' Billy yelled, 'then put the net back over the hole.'

'I d - don't know h - how to?' Winker cried, 'I've n - never d - done owt 1 - like this b - before.'

Billy yelled, 'Lift it up by its back legs and hit it behind its ears, as hard as you can.'

Even as he was speaking, more rabbits began hitting the nets. One or two managed to wriggle their way through to make their run for freedom but were still hampered by the nets. Eddie Green and his brother went scrambling after theirs, whooping like Red Indians,

Billy began to wonder when his turn would come. It was as he pondered this that a rabbit hit his net and began struggling to get out of it. Billy swiftly grabbed it and, extracting it from the net, held it up. It was kicking and struggling and squealing, but he kept hold of it and dispatched it with one blow.

Winker Benton pleaded, 'K - kill m - mine will you, B - Billy?'

Billy turned to see Winker struggling to hold his rabbit. It was kicking and squealing and jerking.

Fixing his net over the hole again he scampered to Winker and grabbed the rabbit off him.

'Here, watch?' he said.

The rabbit was big. It took two blows to kill it. He handed it back to Winker. 'Neck your own from now on.'

As he ran back to his own net he looked round. Percy Green was killing his rabbit and Eddie Green was chasing another one that was still struggling to extricate itself from the net trailing behind it.

After five minutes of frantic activity Billy looked round to see all the gang possessed a least one dead rabbit. Three, he noticed, lay dead beside Wesley's hole and his best pal was chasing a fourth. It was then Hump Bramble came running down the hill waving his arms.

'Somebody's coming?' he yelled.

Billy stared anxiously towards the farm, out of sight beyond the rise of the hill. But, the mist-smeared field was empty.

'I can't see anybody,' he said.

'Course you can't.' shouted Hump. 'You've got to be up the hill where I was.'

Wesley looked wildly around him now. 'Look for the ferret coming out,' he said, 'me dad'll kill me if I lose it.'

Fortunately, almost as soon as Wesley's words were out of his mouth Winker Benton shouted, 'It's h-here.'

He was holding up the yellow eyed, fearsome beast.

'Watch it doesn't bite you,' Billy said.

Wesley ran across the potholed warren and took the animal off Winker and popped it into his sack. With the ferret safely captured, Billy gathered up his nets and his rabbits and stuffed them in his sack. Then, looking round he shouted, 'Let's go.'

Nobody needed prompting.

They bolted along the old track to the bridge leading to the Roman Road. Then they raced past West Hills and on down to Level Lane. It didn't take them long to cover the Lane's distance. Soon they were clambering over the five-barred gate and scampering down the path through Ann Croft. By the time they were running up the hill past the houses at Under Grin, they were really gasping. However, they still found enough wind to labour across Leek Road and into the sanctuary of Grin Wood. Grin Quarry ash tips towered mightily above the screen of trees they sheltered in.

When Billy recovered his breath sufficiently, he looked back over Ann Croft. He said, thankfully, 'I can't see anybody following us.'

Hump Bramble jeered, 'That's because nobody is. I made it up.'

Silence enveloped the gang.

After moments. Billy said, 'What d'you mean, you made it up?'

'Like I said.' Hump shrugged.

Wesley Ward, who was lying on the grass recovering from his long run, now reared up on his elbows and stared at him.

'You mean to tell us we ran all this way because you made it up?'

'That the farmer weren't coming at all?' Eddie Green continued.

'Yes!' Hump said.

'Why?' Billy said presently.

'Because me mum says it's wrong to kill things,' said Hump. 'I always wondered why until now. It was horrible that was.'

'But, they're rabbits,' said Billy.

Wesley got up off the grass, took off his jacket and laid it on the grass and bunched his fists and adopted a boxing posture.

'Put up thee bloody dukes. Hump,' he said, 'I'm going to thump thee.'

Billy got between them and held up his hands. 'Hang on a minute,' he said. He turned to Hump and glared. 'Right, tell us what your mum thinks is so wrong with killing and eating things.'

'She says all life's sacred,' Hump said. 'That's why we're vegetarians,'

'What are vegetarians when they're at home?' Eddie Green said.

'People that don't eat meat.'

'D - don't eat m - meat?' echoed Winker Benton.

It was while this went on that Billy recalled he had never actually seen any sort of meat in Hump's house, or smelt any flesh cooking.

Wesley was saying, 'I've never heard owt so daft in me life.' He slowly pulled on his jacket. 'But it's not worth fighting over.'

Winker Benton said, blinking furiously, 'Even s - so, h - he's spoiled our fun, t - that's for s-sure.'

'Aye,' Eddie Green said fiercely.

At that moment it began to hail, heavily. Billy pulled his coat over his head and cringed and stared up at the leaden sky. He could see white curtains of the stuff drifting towards them from the direction of Axe Edge and The Terret. It was bouncing off the road below covering it rapidly.

Eddie Green said, 'Beggar this, I'm off.'

'And me,' said Percy Green.

Immediately the gang began to disperse, scuttling off down on to Leek Road and running round the bend and down the hill towards Burbage.

Billy felt Wesley's hand cuff his arm.

'What are we for, pal?' he said.

Billy waved the bag holding the dead rabbits and Owd Isaac's nets. 'I've got to drop these nets off at Owd Isaac's first. He wants them tomorrow.'

'Let's go then,' Wesley said.

They found Owd Isaac wasn't in his hut, so Billy left the nets by his shed door. Then he and Wesley ran down Grin Wood on to Holmfield Road. By the time they reached it the hailstorm was over and it was nearly dark, the twilight made all the earlier by the black clouds now scudding across the sky.

Billy grinned. 'So, what dost think of that, pal?'

Wesley returned the smile, his eyes a dazzle of excitement. 'One of your better ideas, mate,' he said,

Holding his bag of rabbits in one hand and his dad's ferret in a bag in the other he added, 'I'll see you at school tomorrow, then.'

Billy nodded, 'Nowt so sure.'

Billy sprinted for home. As he ran, he fingered his penknife in his pocket. He would gut and skin the rabbits for his mum before he went to bed.

The thought of rabbit stew for tomorrow's dinner set his mouth watering. He even began feeling sorry for Hump, not having meat to eat. But the strange thing was Hump didn't seem to mind. Indeed, for a moment or two back in Grin Wood, he got the impression Hump was feeling *sorry for the gang*,

But that was stupid…

CHAPTER ELEVEN

BUSINESS WITH T' WIDOW

Billy was leaning against the Burbage Methodist Chapel wall staring impatiently down Macclesfield Road, Scraggy Bosker was late. Wesley Ward said he would be here at nine o'clock. It was now nearly half-past that hour.

At last Billy saw the horse-drawn vehicle appear round the bend near Burbage Hall lodge and come towards him. But it took another half-minute of steady clip-clopping before Scraggy Bosker drew alongside him and stared down.

'Now then,' he said.

Scraggy was perched on the seat in front of his fruit and vegetable cart. The wares he sold were shelved tent-like behind him from the flat base. A toothy, purple-lipped grin was spread across his round, red face. And from those rubbery lips protruded a worn briar pipe, the bowl of which was badly burnt down the right side, presumably by having matches resting on it while Scraggy lit it.

'Young Billy Nobstick, is it?' Scraggy said, 'Young Wesley said you might be here. Well, I'm always glad of a bit of company so hop up.'

Billy climbed briskly and settled on the bench beside Scraggy. Scraggy smirked down at him and then tugged at his greasy black trilby hat brim and spat an arc of phlegm to the road before he cackled a laugh.

'You're not frightened of me then?' he said.

Billy shook his head, puzzled. 'No.'

'They say I'm a bit of a rum beggar, tha knows,' said Scraggy. 'Or haven't you heard?'

'Yes. I've heard.'

'And it doesn't bother you?'

'No, Wesley Ward said you were all right.'

Scraggy raised his thick brows, 'Did he now? Well, supposing I was to take you up to Flash, and then drop thee off and tell thee to walk back. What would you say to that, eh? I wouldn't be so nice then, would I?'

Billy stared at Scraggy's face, trying to detect whether he was kidding or not. Scraggy did have a reputation for doing daft pranks and Flash was three or four miles away from Burbage – right on top of the moors. Bleak and wind-swept and fit for nowt, most folk said. All you got there was nine months winter and three months bad weather.

'You wouldn't,' he said.

Scraggy arched his brows. 'Why wouldn't I?'

Billy shrugged, 'I don't know,' he said. Then he stared defiantly at Scraggy and just to test if he really was joking he added, 'But, even if you did, I'd still beat that old nag of yours back home by a mile.'

Scraggy burst out laughing. 'Oh, you would, would you, lad?' he said. He chuckled and added, 'Well, tha'll do.' And, as if the matter was settled to his satisfaction, Scraggy cracked the whip near the scruffy, but well-fed carthorse's left ear and called, 'Right, let's have thee. Daisy girl!'

The mare hit the collar. Its hooves scraped on the tarmac road as it strained to get some purchase and set the heavily laden fruit-and-vegetable cart rolling again.

When the outfit was going nicely, hooves clip-clopping on the tarmac, Scraggy leaned over and said, 'Now then, what would you say to a fag? To get us off on t' right footing, so to speak?'

'They make me dizzy,' Billy said.

And there was also the fact that Constable Hastings might see him smoking as they went through the village and the Bobby might tell his mum and dad, or worse still – summons him on the spot for under-age smoking.

Scraggy said, 'I'm not asking you what they do to thee, lad, I'm asking you if you want one.' As he was talking Scraggy put his pipe to one side and lifted a big bacon and egg sandwich out of a brown paper bag that was laid out on the seat beside him. He took a large bite out of it.

'Somebody might see me,' Billy said.

Scraggy's bushy brown eyebrows shot up. 'What if they do?' he said, spitting out a shower of crumbs along with the words.

'Nowt,' said Billy. He decided to lie. 'But I've only just put one out.'

Scraggy sniffed and said, 'Well, suit thee self, lad. Happen you'll have one a bit later on, eh?'

Scraggy wiped a piece of egg off his chin.

'Yes,' Billy said.

As if done with the conversation Scraggy took another bite out of his sandwich and munched on it contentedly as they went passed the School, then the Garage and clip-clopped slowly up Leek Road.

When they got to the cottages further up the road Daisy stopped of her own accord and Scraggy 'harrumphed' and leaned over and shouted, 'I'm here, ladies, your favourite fruit and veg man.'

Within moments a woman poked her head out of one of the upper windows of the nearest cottage. The window wasn't level with the road but Billy could see into it from the cart.

She smiled,

'Oh, it's you, George,' she said. 'Right, weigh me five pounds of potatoes while I make me way up.'

'Your word is my command, my sweet,' said Scraggy beaming a smile.

He climbed down off the cart and began whistling and weighing. While he was doing so the lady appeared at the five-barred gate at the head of the steep lane. Billy saw she was a plump, rosy-cheeked woman with merry eyes. Her frilly pinafore, with flowers printed all over it, added to her already ample bust.

'What are your sprouts like?' she called as she came through the gate.

'Still got the frost on them,' said Scraggy as he tipped the potatoes into the woman's big wicker basket.

The woman rolled her brown eyes. 'Oh, aye? Well, we'll have less of thee flannel for a start. Now then, I'll have the usual... sprouts, carrots and a swede and two pounds of apples. And have you got any fish on?'

'Nice bit of cod,' said Scraggy, weighing carrots. 'It were still swimming in the North Sea at nine o'clock last night.'

'More like last week, if I know you,' said the woman.

'Straight off the train this morning, I tell you,' protested Scraggy; 'prime stuff, direct from Grimsby. It's as fresh as your complexion and as tender as your heart, my love – and would I lie to you?'

The lady rolled her brown eyes again, but Billy could see there was delight in them. 'Oh, go on then, two fillets – but out of the middle mind.'

'Where else, my love?' Scraggy said.

Billy found himself fascinated by the conversation that went on in similar vein for some minutes until the lady's large order was fulfilled, and her next-door neighbour's, who was out.

After cheery goodbyes, Scraggy climbed up on to the cart seat and clicked his tongue.

'Hootcha,' he yelled, 'gerrup, Daisy.' At the command, Daisy nodded, strained, got going again and trotted off towards Canholes.

Pleasing Billy, the sun burst through the clouds and promised to swell out and become a fine, warm day. In fact, Billy began to feel like a king sitting there with Scraggy Bosker on his vegetable cart.

At Canholes more ladies gathered round the cart and Scraggy's jocular banter continued, each fresh customer being showered with endearments and flattery. The same occurred when they reached Grin Row at Ladmanlow. Because of it. Billy recalled Wesley Ward saying only last week – and he got it from his dad – Scraggy Bosker had the reputation of being 'a bit of a lady's man'. Whatever that meant.

Half an hour later they were clattering over the railway crossing and clopping up Leek Rood, passing Stanley Moor Reservoir on the left.

As they climbed steadily up Axe Edge and past The Terret, the sun's heat began to feel really warm on Billy. He relaxed. He was really looking forward to the rest of the day, travelling with Scraggy Bosker on his fruit and veg cart. Wesley was right; Scraggy Bosker was good company. As they climbed diagonally up and along the side of Axe Edge, Scraggy nudged him and nodded behind him and winked.

'So, what d'you make of 'em?' he said,

Billy looked up and frowned. 'Who?'

'Them ladies,' Scraggy said.

'They're all right, I suppose.'

'Friendly like, eh?' said Scraggy.

'Yes.'

'Trouble is,' Scraggy said, 'that's all they are ... friendly.'

Billy frowned. 'What's wrong with being friendly?'

Scraggy looked at him askance. 'Nowt lad, but there's friendly and *friendly*, if you know what I mean.'

'No, I don't.'

Scraggy raised his brows. 'No, I suppose tha doesn't. How old did you say you was?'

'Ten.'

'I see. Well, there's no point in going on, is there?'

'Why not?'

Scraggy didn't answer. But Billy found he was curious, however he let it be – it was too nice a day to be curious – and turned to stare back at the peaceful scene they were leaving behind them.

In the sunshine he could see railway lines shining in the sun; rows of washing pegged out in front of the gritstone, grey-slated cottages of Grin Row. Lining the side of Parks Lane he could see large heaps of dirty-white lime waste. Piles of it also surrounded the Sidings and Wagon Shops and all the other buildings belonging to Grin Quarry. There was so much of the waste it was banked up on the side of the road. And the limekilns that were lined up above Parks Lane looked like obese black giants in the brilliant sunlight. Billy could see the dark smoke belching out of them in thick black columns and swirling away towards Harpur Hill. Billy hoped the ladies in that village didn't have any washing out. If they did, it would be ruined.

Scraggy grinned down at him and let go of the reins – which he was holding loosely, anyway – and pulled out his pipe. He commenced to cut tobacco from the black plug in his hand and rub it into flake before he tamped it down into his scarred briar. He began lighting it. As he puffed a loaded lorry came grinding in bottom gear up the hill behind them. As the vehicle drew level with them, the driver honked his horn and leaned across the engine cowling in the cab and peered out through the nearside open window.

'Hey up, Scraggy,' he yelled. 'Are t' all right?'

Scraggy looked sideways at him, and paused in lighting his pipe. 'Course I am. Where are you off to then, Fred?'

'Burslem.'

'Pot country?' Scraggy grinned. 'Well, go steady down Upper Hulme and when tha gets t' Burslem don't do anything I wouldn't do.' He grinned and spat down on to the road.

The lorry driver called, 'Thee too. Sunshine. So, how about an apple?'

Scraggy leaned back and selected one and tossed it through the lorry's cab window.

'That's a pint you owe me.'

Fred waved, 'See you in The Swan Saturday night.'

'Aye, and don't forget,' said Scraggy.

The lorry roared past. Billy saw it was loaded with bagged lime, wrapped in a dirty tarpaulin, which had Taylor Frith and Sons painted on it.

'Stinking things they are,' Scraggy said as the lorry drew away from them, 'they ought to be banned.'

'Daisy doesn't seem to mind them,' Billy said. He was still having bad memories of Jerusalem's Cuckoo – his best mate's donkey, or was – and its reaction to noise. In particular the barking of Barton's mongrel dog which caused it to bolt through the village.

'Oh, aye,' Scraggy said, 'she's placid enough is Daisy. Nowt much disturbs her, I can tell thee.'

He puffed contentedly on his pipe for a while and then fumbled in the pocket of his thick black overcoat and pulled out a packet of Player's Navy Cut cigarettes. He opened it and selected one and then looked down.

'D'you want that fag now?' he said.

'Yeh,' Billy said.

'Get a hold of it then,' Scraggy said, waving the cigarette under his nose.

Billy took the offered Player's. He could cope with smoking cigarettes all right; it was Owd Isaac's pigtail twist that made him feel poorly. He wasn't going to have any more of that stuff in a hurry. He still held horrible memories of throwing up in front of Owd Isaac during the Summer Holidays after smoking that foul tobacco.

Scraggy pulled out a box of Swan Vestas. He took a match out and lighted it, and then he pulled his unbuttoned overcoat out to shield the match flame against being blown out by the breeze that was bustling down off The Terret.

'Here, duck in here and get her lit,' he said.

Billy leaned over into the shelter of the coat and began puffing. Soon the cigarette was lighted. And, as usual, he coughed and went dizzy. But he managed to hide any further feelings of nausea. The dizziness, he knew, would soon wear off with it only being a cigarette.

After fifteen minutes of steady clopping and the passing and honking of two more lorries, Scraggy turned the horse off the main road and down the steep lane to Brandside. From here on there were lots of ups and downs and the need to make detours up winding lanes before stopping to gossip and sell vegetables and fish to ladies at the gates and track ends of remote homesteads. Often Scraggy needed to bellow at Daisy and crack the whip over her head to keep her moving. Once or twice Billy and Scraggy were even obliged to get off the cart and walk alongside it to ease the horse's heavy burden. One time they had to get behind and push the hill was so steep. When they reached the first cottages of Flash Scraggy pulled out his big pocket watch and said, beaming down at him, 'Bang on time, lad. You're got to be regular, tha knows. T' ladies expect it.'

Scraggy parked outside the New Inn pub, stood up and yelled, 'It's Scraggy, ladies.'

Soon the village women came out of their cottages. They carefully inspected the wares Scraggy was carrying. Some passed clinical judgment on a few items, but with liberal sprinklings of jolly banter and soothing assurances, Scraggy turned their doubts into guarded enthusiasm and served them all efficiently. But Billy found Scraggy's arrival in the hamlet started a right gossipy get together amongst the ladies. In fact the housewives were still talking as Scraggy climbed up on to the cart, waved a fond farewell, and urged Daisy out of the village and down towards Gradbach.

At a cottage half a mile down the road a plump woman in a flowery coverall came out to the roadside. A Welsh collie hovered round her heels, its pink tongue lolling, its speckled eyes appraising. She smiled and offered Scraggy a large, piping hot meat and potato pie. In exchange Scraggy sorted out some vegetables and fruit and passed them down to her with a grin.

'There you are, m'love,' he said. 'Fair exchange is no robbery as they say.'

'Mind how you go,' the lady called cheerfully.

'Nowt so sure,' said Scraggy, with a grin.

As they clopped on, Scraggy offered Billy half the pie.

'Here, get that down thee neck,' he said, 'Tha won't find a better-tasting pie than that, no matter where you go.'

Billy needed no prompting; he was ravenous. He devoured the pie with relish. When he finished Scraggy tossed him an apple he picked out of a box behind him. 'There, round it off with that, lad,' he said. Then he looked worriedly at the sky. 'I don't like the look of those clouds.'

Billy looked up. He saw big, black-bellied clouds scurrying above the ridge of bracken-covered and sheep dotted hills to their right.

'Oh, heck,' he said, 'I haven't got me coat.'

Scraggy said, 'Oh, don't fret about that, lad. We'll find you summat for thee to cover up with. Like as not it'll just pass over.'

It did. Billy now found the hurrying variations of sunlight and cloud-shadow leaping and bounding over the green and rust-coloured moorland fascinating. Indeed, he decided, the various cloud shapes looked like galloping horses as they chased and leapt over wild, vast slopes and down narrow bilberry bush choked ravines.

After more calls on farmhouses and cottages. Scraggy finally steered the cart up on to the Leek-Buxton Road, about a quarter of a mile below the Royal Cottage Inn. The fruit and vegetables and fish were now sold, except for some prime stuff Scraggy selected and set aside earlier in the day.

Because the cart was now so much lighter Daisy began to trot briskly up the road towards Buxton. It was clear she knew the round backwards.

As they jogged along, Scraggy leaned over. 'I'll be calling on t' widow now, lad,' he said with a smirk,

Billy cocked his ears up at the word 'widow'. He immediately pictured a severe woman dressed in an ankle length black frock and laced up black boots, and with a sharp hooked nose and piercing black eyes. That was how they were at the cinema, anyway – or was it 'spinsters' who were supposed to look like that? Or maybe it was 'housekeepers', or was it 'witches'?

'Oh,' he said,

'A very refined woman is t' widow, lad,' Scraggy said. 'Mine host at the Tippler's Arms.'

'Is she?'

'Oh, aye,' said Scraggy with gravity.

In a short while The Tippler's Arms came into view. A low, ancient-looking hostelry set back off the bleak moorland road.

Billy shrunk into his shabby, patched jacket, hoping this wasn't going to take long. For, by now, the sun was set and the air was growing cooler by the minute and dark clouds were lowering and scraping along the high, ragged skyline. The gloom made the moorland around look ghostly, even menacing. Indeed, Billy decided, some of the rock formations they passed appeared to be really scary from certain angles, especially when the mists dropped to play amongst their grotesque shapes.

At the Tippler's Arms Scraggy turned the cart off the rood and guided it into the yard at the rear of the pub. There, Scraggy eased Daisy to a stop. Then he hopped down and went to the rear of the cart. He was soon back carrying a nosebag half-full of oats.

While talking softly to Daisy, Scraggy gently placed the bag over her nose. The mare began to munch contentedly on the oats.

Billy now noticed a change in Scraggy. He seemed to be more alert and there was definitely a sparkle in his eyes. And he appeared to be tingling with anticipation. He straightened his red silk scarf. He dusted down his coat. Then he looked at the black-painted back door of the pub.

'Margaret, my treasure,' he called; 'I'm here.'

Billy was surprised to see a shapely, smiling woman appear at the rear door of the Inn. She didn't look a bit like the widows his fantasies recently conjured up. Indeed, he found 'Margaret, my treasure' possessed corn-coloured hair, which was piled up like a Coburg loaf on top of her head. She was, he also saw, clothed in a frilly white blouse and a light-blue skirt. And a broad, patent leather black belt circled her narrow waist. A big shiny buckle fastened it. She was also wearing bright red lipstick on her fulsome lips, which, Billy decided, made her look like his sister's play doll, before the paint wore off that is. Nevertheless, she was as beautiful as any of the film stars he saw at the picture houses down Buxton.

'Are the apples nice, Georgy?' she cooed.

'Morning gathered, my love,' Scraggy said, 'just for you.'

The woman giggled, then Billy saw her face drop as her blue gaze fell on him. It was as though she was seeing him for the first time. There was horror on her face. 'Oh, dear, Georgy,' she said, 'is that a boy? You can't bring him in here. That won't do, will it? Not just now.'

Scraggy grinned. 'He'll be all right on t' cart, my love,' he said. 'He's just along for a bit of company,' Scraggy looked up, grinning. 'Aren't you, lad?'

'Yes.'

'Well, that's all right then,' said 'Margaret, my treasure'. 'It wouldn't do to have a boy in here, would it?'

'Certainly not, petal,' Scraggy said. Then he whispered, 'I won't be long, lad, maybe an hour, no more. I'll fix up the tarpaulin for you and I'll see tha gets a cup of tea and a bit o' cake. That'll be all right for thee, won't it?'

Billy looked miserably at the sky. Night was setting in now and it was getting very cold. He wanted to be heading for home but on the other hand he didn't want to upset Scraggy. He might not invite him along again.

He said. 'I'll be all right, Mr Bosker.'

'Aye, 'course tha will, lad,' Scraggy said.

He quickly erected a frame over the cart and draped a tarpaulin over it. Across the tarp was stencilled Clay Cross in white paint. When Scraggy finished manoeuvring the sheet into place he beamed him a smile. 'Now then, lad; tha'll be as snug as a bug in a rug in there.'

Billy peered from under the tarpaulin and watched Scraggy trot gleefully off into the rear of the pub. Scraggy was carrying the vegetables and fruit he so carefully put aside earlier on in the day. True to his word, ten minutes later, he came out carrying a steaming mug of tea and a big slab of fruitcake.

'There you are, lad,' he said, 'get that down thee.'

Billy relieved him of the food and watched Scraggy sprint back into the pub. Soon a light came on and 'Margaret my love' drew the curtains. Soon Billy could hear laughing, the rattle of knives and forks on plates. Half an hour later the light downstairs dimmed and light from an oil lamp bloomed out of one of the tiny windows upstairs. T' widow once more drew the curtains and not long after that, *that light* went out.

Billy stared gloomily at the dark frame of the window before he hunkered down into his coat to wait. It seemed ages passed before a light downstairs brightened up again. Then Billy heard more laughing and talking. Presently, Scraggy appeared at the door, his face red and shiny. The widow, Billy observed, was with him. She was smiling radiantly and her ample arms were folded across her breasts. But her hair wasn't neat any more. Wisps of it were hanging out.

Halfway across the yard Scraggy turned to wave. The widow blew lots of kisses.

'Next week, my petal?' Scraggy called.

'I can't wait,' said the widow.

Billy pretended not to listen. This was what they must call courting.

As Scraggy crossed the rest of the yard Billy noticed that his rolling gait was now even unsteadier – the type of walk Billy observed half-drunken men adopt. And Scraggy had a silly grin on his face.

However, he managed to light a couple of lamps he fumbled out of the box built into the back of the cart. He hung the red lamp at the back and the clear one at the front. 'We need to be seen, lad,' he said, his voice now a thick slur, 'even though t' traffic won't be much.'

Then he hiccupped twice and climbed erratically on to the cart. Aboard, he leaned close. Billy could smell beer and onions on his breath and there was also a strong suggestion of lady's perfume there, too.

'It pays to keep well in with Mine Host, lad,' Scraggy said presently. He tapped the side of his nose with a stubby finger. 'Especially out of licensing hours.'

'Oh,' Billy said. He was cold and fed up. 'What about this cup and plate?'

Scraggy looked bleary-eyed at the utensils in Billy's hand, 'Don't worry about them, lad. I'll see Mine Host gets them back next week.'

Giggling he fumbled in one of his large overcoat pockets and pulled out a new packet of Players. 'Here, get yourself another fag, lad,' he said and hiccupped. 'Warm thee nose up, eh?'

Bill took the cigarette and lighted it off the match Scraggy struck, though he did have to chase the light around a little, due to Scraggy's unsteady demeanour. When the cigarette was lighted Scraggy wafted out the match and tossed the dead stick into the dark. 'Right, lad,' he said, 'I'm just going to have a lie down in the back off cart now if you don't mind.'

Billy stared, despondency flooding through him. 'I thought we were going home?'

Scraggy's brows shot up. 'And so we are, lad,' he said. 'Good old Daisy'll see to that. Her's one in a thousand is our Daisy.'

Scraggy now leaned over the side of the cart and pressing each side of his nose in turn expelled phlegm out of each passageway. The residue of the mucus he flicked off the end of his nose before wiping his hand on the breast of his coat. 'That's better,' he said. He flapped the reins. 'Now then. Daisy girl,' he called, 'take us home.'

Daisy obediently nodded her head and strained into the collar and began to walk easily out of the yard. On the main road she turned towards Buxton.

Scraggy sighed and laid down the reins over the seat and flopped down in the back of the cart and rested his head on a half-full sack of potatoes. He folded his arms, closed his eyes and curled up.

'Hop off when we get to Burbage, lad,' he said.

Within two minutes, soft snores came.

Billy peered around the side of the tarpaulin. He puffed on his fag. The hills were black, towering humps swelling like elephants' backs above the road. Here and there he saw inviting yellow oil lamplight coming from the isolated farms and homesteads that were scattered over this wild Staffordshire-Derbyshire moorland. Rain began to beat out of the night.

He pulled in his head and listened to it patter against the side of the tarpaulin. But the steady clip-clop of Daisy's hooves on the road was reassuring. He leaned back and allowed his head to roll with the steady movement of the cart. All in all, he decided, it had been a great day. He silently thanked his best pal Wesley Ward for putting him on to Scraggy Bosker. Maybe Scraggy would take him with him again. He'd done nothing to upset him.

Meanwhile, Daisy headed unerringly for home.

CHAPTER TWELVE

HOT POT SUPPER

Half past eight in the evening. Another five days and it would be Christmas Day. Happy though tired, Billy finished three hours of chopping and bundling sticks. Scampering out of the yard he ran down Leek Road, buttoning up his heavy Melton overcoat.

The coat was lovely and warm. Mrs Matchless – the married daughter of Mr Belham, the newsagent – passed it on to his mum a fortnight ago. Mrs Matchless said it was now too small for her own son, Charlie, but there was still plenty of wear in it and it seemed such a waste of a good coat to have it sitting there in the wardrobe getting moth-eaten – despite the liberal presence of mothballs – so she passed it on to his mum.

Happy with his good fortune Billy began sliding on his hobnail boots down the black ribbon of ice-covered road, stretching away into the night before him – punctuated only by the yellow pools of gas lamplight. The mellow amber glows glittered on the icicles that hung from the hedges and trees and roof gutters, making it a magic wonderland for Billy as he went gliding past them.

Gazing at the enchanted night, Billy now decided snow was on the way. He could feel it in the air. And that would mean sledging down Doghole or Temple Fields; snowball fights; roasting chestnuts and earning a bob or two ridding people's drives and paths of snow.

He began to plot what he would do with the extra money he would earn. He would buy more Christmas presents for people he couldn't afford to buy for at the moment. And one Christmas job was already

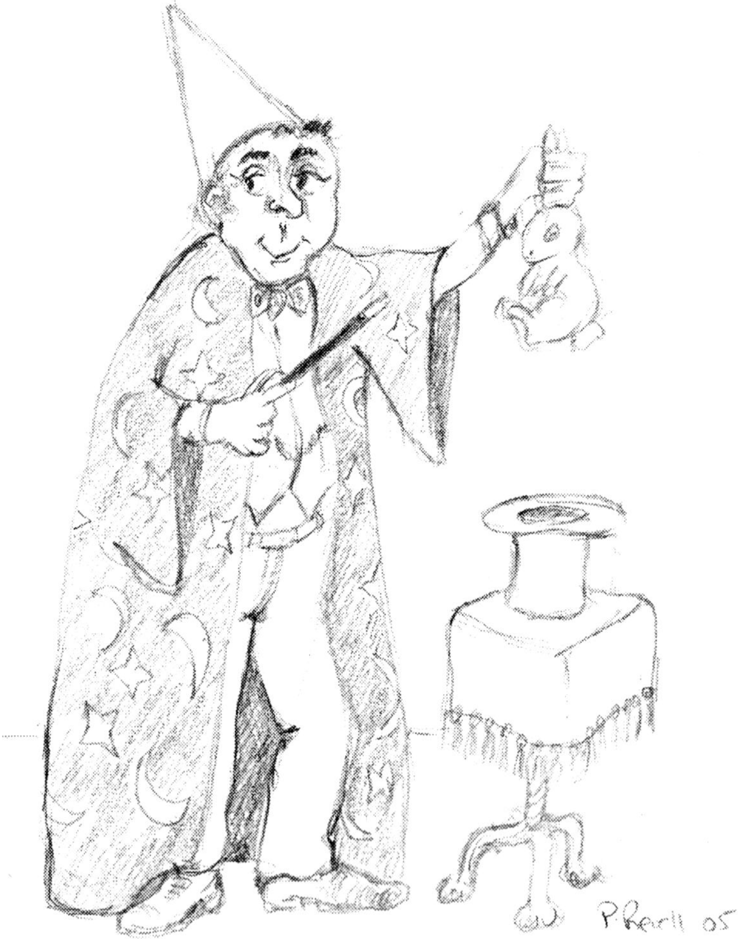

done. Last week, at home, he helped hang up the paper chains they'd been making since October… and the crepe paper bells that were bought from the Woolworths sale two years ago. After that they decorated the Christmas tree, using the tinsel and baubles saved from last year.

But Christmas day was the best, Billy decided. On Christmas day there would be an orange and an apple in his stocking and granddad's usual present of short, brown corduroy trousers (to see him through the school year) would be ceremoniously handed over. Then there would be Aunt Olivers present. She usually knitted him a pullover. There would be the usual pair of socks from his Uncle Fred. But, best of all, his mum and dad promised him, if he was very good, they would see about buying him the Hornby train set he saw down Buxton in Elliot's Toy Shop, situated at the bottom of Spring Gardens; the train that went round and round in a circle.

When he reached the end of the road leading to his house he scooted up the hill and eagerly burst in through the front door. Pulling aside the draught curtain he entered the living room. Turning quickly he shut the door again and drew the draught curtain back into place and replaced the sausage across the bottom of the door.

When he looked into the living room he found his mum was sitting on the settee, sewing another patch on to his school trousers. A coal fire flickered warmly in the grate. The lighted single gaslight was hissing above. His granddad was in his big armchair in the corner, doing his crossword. His father was snoring in his chair in the other corner, his mouth wide open. Sister Mary would be in bed, Billy guessed. She was only six years old and needed her sleep. His brother Luke would be still at work at the Spa Cinema down Buxton. He knew it would be turned eleven before he got in.

His cheeks already glowing with the warmth in the room he stripped off his black Melton overcoat and hung it up on one of the four coat hooks at the bottom of the stairs. Coming back into the room his mum said, 'You're late.'

She didn't look up from her sewing.

'I stayed on a bit.'

'Is he paying you extra for it?'

'Yes. A bob over and maybe a Christmas bonus.'

'That's all right then,' his mother said, straightening the patch she was sewing. 'Well, your supper's on the hob; I've saved you some neck of mutton stew.'

Billy's mouth watered. It was one of his favourite foods.

His granddad looked up and smiled, 'That stuff'll stick to thee ribs, lad. Just what you need for tomorrow night, carolling with t' choir if this cold weather keeps up.'

Billy's elation dropped like a stone. He'd forgot about that.

'Do I have to go?' he muttered. 'I'm supposed to be going carol singing with the gang tomorrow night.'

His granddad's stare, when it reached him, was pained. 'Of course you have to, lad,' he said. 'It's a good fundraiser for the church. You can always go carolling with the gang another night.'

'But we arranged to go tomorrow,' said Billy. It would be extra money to buy more presents.

His granddad rustled his newspaper 'You heard what the vicar said on Sunday, lad; about this being the time of the birth of our Lord? It's the greatest celebration in the Christian calendar. You must know that?'

'But I promised,' Billy said.

'The Church needs all the money it can get, lad,' his granddad said. 'It enables us to fund the missionaries and feed the poor in the cities. It's our duty to do all we can for those unfortunate people. It spreads the Gospel, too. You know the vicar expects a full turn out. What's more, Burbage Silver Prize Band will be going round with us.'

'But it's not fair,' Billy said.

'Do as your granddad tells you,' his mum said sharply.

'But I promised the gang,' said Billy and added, 'I'm getting fed up of going to church.'

'You're not going to church,' his mother emphasised, 'you're going carol singing, so that's the end of it.'

'But it's always me,' Billy said.

'No it isn't,' said his mum. 'Now shut up and get on with your supper or it'll be upstairs with nowt in your belly.'

Mumbling Billy got his stew off the hob and placed it on a pad on the tiny table by the flowery curtains drawn across the front window. After that he went into the kitchen and reached a dessertspoon out of the cutlery box, returned and settled down to eat his supper while casting sulky glances at his mum. In the silence, the gas lamp in the centre of the ceiling continued to hiss. Presently, his granddad began to fiddle with the wireless. It whistled and squeaked and crackled a few times before the announcer's voice came into full focus: 'This is the Nine o'clock News.'

His granddad sat back and placed his hands in a prayer formation under his chin while he listened gravely to every word that was said.

There was nothing but bad news these days his granddad told him the other day. Billy knew his granddad was very troubled by it all. His granddad said it looked like Britain would soon be at war with the Hun again, despite Prime Minister Neville Chamberlain's assurances there would be peace in our time. But his dad said Herr Hitler (whoever he was) needed teaching a lesson and they should get on with doing it. But instead The Prime Minister had to go to Munich, and come back waving that piece of useless paper claiming the crisis was over. Herr Hitler was a liar and a bully, his dad raged, and should be treated like one.

The newsreader's voice droned on. Billy ate his supper, relishing the flavours of the neck of mutton. The stew – as well as having meat and bone in it – was full of potato, swede, onion, carrots, and parsnips: all grown in his granddad's allotments, which he helped to till and set.

Billy ate ravenously, his round, pale face beginning to glow as the warmth of the stew soaked into his frost-pinched cheeks. But eating the stew set his mind recalling the Hot Pot Supper held last week in the Methodist Hall at the back of the Chapel. He thought he would have missed the feast this year after his dad lost his job Pumping The Organ. But he didn't.

Billy dreamed on, the memories of the Hot Pot Supper flooding back. The big, hot room with the curtained stage at the top end; the steamy kitchen off to the right of the entrance door, the women laughing and chatting noisily inside it. The long trestle tables on which – besides cutlery and dishes – stood huge enamel washbasins with vast brown crusts over the top of them. The long rows of children sitting at the tables, all scrubbed and rosy-cheeked; the girls in pretty dresses and with coloured ribbons in their hair. The boys, their hair slicked down with solid brilliantine, dressed in their Very Best Clothes, their stockings pulled up and kept in place with elastic bands. And the women, standing by the immense pies on the tables... each wore a cheery grin on their flushed red faces and beamed with delight at the sight of so many excited, happy children. It was clear the ladies were enjoying the children's joy as much as their own.

Now Mr Goodfellow, the preacher, asked for silence. The place went hushed and Mr Goodfellow said prayers, thanking the Lord for his bounty. Everybody said 'amen' and then the swell of voices rose again as the ladies broke open the vast piecrusts. As they did a huge cheer went up from the children and steam arose and delicious aromas began to permeate the already stifling air.

Soon the ladies, with big wooden spoons, were ladling out the feast on to the large plates, which were already stacked by their sides. 'Pass them on,' they kept saying, 'pass them on,' their eyes bright with happiness.

Before long each child had a plate full of the marvellous food set before them and they began to tuck in with relish after Mr Goodfellow, seated at the head of the table, waved his spoon and said, 'Eat up, children. Eat up. Don't stand on ceremony.'

The meal served, the ladies retired to have their meal in the kitchen. Soon laughter came from there and a continuous hubbub of light-hearted chatter.

After the raspberry jelly dessert they were each given an orange and a cracker. Billy pocketed his orange (the first orange he'd had this year) to eat later before pulling his cracker with Wesley Ward. Inside his cracker Billy found a red paper hat, all rolled up with an elastic band round it, which he opened and pulled over his short, brown, curly hair. Also there was a tin whistle in the cracker on which he tried to play some tunes, but he wasn't very successful. Wesley, with equal excitement, found a frog clicker in his cracker and a green hat. Wesley clicked the frog constantly, usually in peoples' ears. In Winker Benton's cracker were a pink hat and a small pack of playing cards. In Hump Bramble's was a set of cardboard dominoes. The Green brothers got good presents, too. The meal eaten and the crackers opened, they were all asked to move to the sides of the hall (taking their chairs with them) while the trestle tables were cleared and dismantled by the men and the bigger boys and stacked under the stage. Then came the games.

The first one they played was Musical Chairs and Billy won. He beat Monica Pane to the last chair. She stalked off, her arms straight down and pressed tight against the sides of her blue dress with the big white bow at the back.

When she reached her chair she turned and put her tongue out at him before sticking her nose up in the air and disdainfully looking away. The prize was announced as being a box of Basset's Liquonce Allsorts, which he duly went up and accepted. But somehow, he felt bad about beating Monica to the last chair and later on gave her four of the sweets. The ones he didn't like; the ones with coconut flakes clustered around a liquorice core. When he handed them to her, her eyes lit up and she even smiled at him. 'Oh, I love these ones, Billy,' she said.

He found he didn't know whether to be pleased about that or not. He rather hoped she didn't like them.

Then came games of Blind Man's Bluff, Pass The Parcel, I Spy. And all the while, in the background, was the clatter of pots and pans being washed up amid gales of laughter. It came from the ladies working in the kitchen.

After an hour of games Mr Goodfellow got up on to the stage. His round face flushed, he held his hands aloft. His kind eyes smiled down at them. He seemed to be enjoying the party as much as anybody. But when Mr Goodfellow did step up the women who were organising the games began hissing, 'Shush, children, quiet. Please.'

Gradually silence descended on the hall.

'And now, boys and girls,' said Mr Goodfellow, 'I want you all to show your appreciation of the good ladies who yearly make this event such a memorable occasion.'

He motioned with a hand to the women who were now ranked – red and rosy – at the back of the hall. 'Each year,' went on Mr Goodfellow, 'they give of their time – freely and generously – to make these Suppers such happy – and, may I say? – tasty affairs. And this year, 1938 – is yet another triumph, perhaps better even than all the previous ones. What would we do without them boys and girls? I shudder to think. We would certainly be the poorer without their generosity of spirit and their steadfast assistance.' Mr Goodfellow held up his hands again. 'So, now, will you all give three of the biggest cheers you can manage – just for them. Are you ready? Hip, hip…'

'Hooray!" chorused die children

'Hip, hip…'

'Hooray!'

'Hip, hip…'

'Hoooooray!'

For the last cheer Billy took a huge breath and yelled his heart out, so excited and happy was he. And the cheers went on, interspersed with whistles of delight while all the ladies smiled and looked surprised, or amazed, or flattered, but mainly clearly delighted by the response. Mr Goodfellow eventually had to hold his hands up for quiet.

'Thank you, thank you., thank you, children, for that excellent show of gratitude,' he said. 'But…' he raised his hands again and waited for the noise to die down '…the fun isn't over yet.'

Gasps of surprise.

'Shush, shush,' called the ladies.

'Now,' said Mr Goodfellow, 'I want you all to get a chair each and form them into rows – as quietly as you can – facing the stage and then sit down. For next we have Wizzo the Wizard who, this evening, has come all the way from Fairfield, especially to entertain us.'

More excited whoops went up and with Wesley Ward and Winker Benton, Hump Bramble and the Green brothers, Billy joined in the feverish activity of moving the chairs. The gang managed to arrange their chairs along the front row. When the noises subsided, the electric lights in the hall were switched off. Only the foot lights across the stage were kept on.

Mr Goodfellow raised his hand once more. 'And so, children,' he said; 'a huge round of applause for Wizzo the Wizard!'

He held his hand out and the curtains parted and, as he went offstage, he shouted once more, 'Wizzo the Wizard, boys and girls! Give him a good old Burbage cheer!'

Huge whoops rent the air – Billy thought his yell was the loudest of the lot – and out on to the front of the stage stepped a short fat man with a very tall, conical red hat on his head. He also wore a black cloak with silver stars and moons all over it. In his hand was a long black wand with a white tip.

'Good evening, children!' he called.

Everybody shouted back, excitedly, 'Good evening.'

It was then the lady came on to the stage carrying a small table on which was a black cloth and a top hat.

'My very able assistant, Miss Nancy Faircross,' said the wizard, beaming across the footlights.

More cheers went up.

The lady fascinated Billy. She was wearing a sparkling green dress with only a short skirt to it. On her fat legs she wore long black stockings that looked as though they were made from a fishing net. And it was obvious her blonde hair had been freshly permed. She was smiling; her lips bright red with lipstick and around her eyes was the black stuff his mum called mascara. The lady rubbed her legs together and waved a hand towards Wizzo the Wizard as she stepped back to the side of the stage.

'Wizzo the Wizard, boys and girls,' she called, 'will now entertain you.'

There came the amazing display of magic.

Billy was aware of wizards, but thought they weren't really real, just in books. But when Wizzo the Wizard began pulling fans of cards out of the air, and out of the sparkly lady's bosom and from behind her ear, and then began producing bottle after bottle from only one bottle on the table, and then pulling doves out of his clothing and out of thin air, and then putting them on a perch the lady brought on stage. Billy had no doubts he was in the presence of a magician of the highest order. Perhaps the best in the world. But the show wasn't over. Wizzo the Wizard now picked up the top hat from the tiny table and showed it to the audience, tipping it upside down, waving it about. It was definitely empty; Billy was certain of that and Wesley agreed. Then the wizard wafted the hat close to his cloak before putting it back on the table and covering it with a cloth again. He stared out across the footlights.

'And now, children,' he said, flourishing his magic stick, 'as a grand finale to an evening of superb entertainment I will attempt to do the impossible – produce a real live rabbit from thin air!'

More gasps of wonder and buzzes of excitement came as Wizzo the Wizard tapped the top of the top hat with his stick and called 'Abracadabra! Ooka Balooo!' Then he put his hand in and pulled out a white rabbit with startling pink eyes and cuddled it to his chest.

'Wallah,' he exclaimed. 'The impossible has been achieved!'

Gasps of amazement filled the hall. Then everybody shrieked and whooped and cheered while The Great Wizzo took bow after bow, before, clearly reluctantly, walking off the stage.

However, the cheers continued and he came back looking surprised that more bows were being called for. And the sparkly lady took her bows too before the curtains were finally pulled together and Mr Goodfellow came on to the stage once more.

'And now, children,' he said, with a hint of sadness in his voice, 'it is time to bring the festivities to a close. I want to thank you all so much for coming and making this event such a joyous occasion. But, before you go, each one of you will receive a small bag of sweets on your way out.' He waved, 'Now God bless you all and may the Lord keep you safe in the troubled times that seem to lie ahead.'

This time the roof nearly lifted off as cheer after cheer went up....

'Right – off to bed with you,. Billy,' his mum said. 'You can do your dreaming upstairs.'

The memories of the Hot Pot supper dissolved. Billy looked at the empty bowl before him. While he reminisced, he'd eaten all his stew.

He stared at his mum.

'Can't I stay up a bit?' he said. 'It's nearly Christmas.'

'What difference does that make – nearly Christmas?' his mum said. 'You still need your rest. You'll never be up to do you paper round in the morning.'

Billy didn't argue. He really was tired. He just felt he had to try it on, that's all. He rose from the table and got his green-enamel candleholder and lighted the half-burnt-down candle in it with one of the paper spills in the polished brass shell casing standing in the tiled hearth, which his granddad brought back from the Great War.

He lighted it

He went up the two flights of stairs to the attic.

Slowly he stripped off his patched jacket and jersey, unclipped his snake belt and took off his short grey flannel trousers. He pulled his nightshirt over his naked body. Because of the razor-sharp cold in the bedroom huge goose pimples began to form all over his body. His skin quivered. But before he climbed into bed he went to the window and breathed on one of the frost-covered panes. Then, to make the hole large enough to see through, he completed the process by licking the glass.

To his delight he saw snow was beginning fall, driven before the blustering wind. It was hitting the windowpane and racing like geese down across the light from the gas lamp outside the house. It was already settling on the knapped road and tarmac pavement below.

His evening was complete. He climbed into the squeaking iron frame bed with the brass knobs and pulled the blankets over him and curled into a ball and lay shivering until the heat of his body warmed the bedding. Then he settled flat on his back and put his hands behind his head and stared at the pictures on the ceiling, cast there by the light from the gas lamp outside. As usual there were ships and castles and animals, as real as they could be.

Billy dreamed on. With the money he would hopefully get snow ridding paths and drives and the money he expected to get from going with the gang carol singing the day after tomorrow, and some money he had already saved, he should be able to buy good presents this year. A big handkerchief for his granddad, a packet of ten Park Drive cigarettes for his dad, a little broach for his sister, bought out of Woolworths down Buxton, maybe a handkerchief for his brother Luke. For his mum a special present: there was a shop in Buxton that sold these small milky white glass swans. They were in the window –

all shiny, their necks gracefully bowed, their black eyes gazing into the blue base they appeared to be swimming on. Yes, that's what he would get for his mum, because she was the best mum of all. And he wouldn't forget to buy her a Christmas card, either.

He snuggled down and closed his eyes. Outside, the snow swirled out of the black sky and whipped across the barren moors where sheep cowered under walls, heather banks and in deep hollows. And like mischievous white imps the flakes also waltzed in crazily spinning spirals along the now deserted iced-over streets of the village and piled into ever heightening drifts against walls and fences.

The Peakland snows were here.

Billy sank slowly into happy sleep.